YES, WE ARE STILL PRAISING BILL PRYST

"Like my first gang bang. Bill Pryst's latest work left me satisfied, sore, and slightly ashamed." - North Westchester Hourly Review

"Someone must have owed him a shit load of money to publish this piece of garbage." - South Beach Central Literary Workshop

"The way I look at it, sex and violence are both fun, so long as they're enjoyed separately. I try to live my life by that motto." - Ron Stapleton – Rape Councilor

"I don't give a shit about the book. I just want him inside me." - Gloria Steinman

"Ever have a funky taste in your mouth after a night of drinking and eating sour pussy? That's what it's like." - Moe Barot

"The cover's mesmerizing. Everything after that was a letdown." - Caesar Robenga

"I want to give him my virginity like a box of chocolates on Valentine's Day. Warm, milky and sugary, all the way down." - Phillis Green

AND...

"Bill Pryst is the Rottweiler on the jugular of the American publishing industry." - Steimer & Steimer Publishing House

"Van Gogh meant to send Bill his ear, but there was a mix up at the post office." - Remy Smithson - Historian

"Dude, that donkey is hung like Bill Pryst!" - Jerry Weiss

"Bill Pryst is to literature what Doctor Mengela was to pediatrics." - Boston Bostonian - Starred Review

"...with prose as elegant as a meth addict beating his wife." - West Belfast Review

"Bill Pryst is not gay, okay? He just likes getting his dick sucked." - Lawrence "Laura" McGillicutty – Sing Sing Maximum Security Prison, Prisoner #166598

"No, for the last time, Bill Pryst is not a registered gynecologist." - Dr. Smith Bregard, MD

WE'RE DONE.

Rick Glacier: PI
in
FIST
FULL OF
BRUNETTES

A Multiple-Choice Thriller

BY BILL PRYST

FIRST FINNEAN NILSEN PROJECTS EDITION – AUGUST 2011

This book is a work of fiction. Literally. Nothing about this book is real except for the fact that it exists. Resemblance to people, alive or dead, or places, past or present, is purely coincidental. All names are fictitious, including those in the "Praise for Bill Pryst" section, the cover page, and in the "About" sections.

ISBN: 0615501311
ISBN-13: 9780615501314

ACKNOWLEDGEMENTS

It is very rare for a book to be the work of one, single individual. With any finished novel there are legions of people behind the scenes that seldom receive any credit. There are type-setters and cover designers, marketing professionals and sales people who make the book a success. There are countless individuals who give, thanklessly, hours upon hours of their time so that the author can be well schooled on all the intricate details of some little piece that not one reader notices but must none-the-less be exhaustively researched.

This book would be the exception. It's mine. All mine. I did the work, wrote it without any help. I deserve all the credit. All the praise. Everything. Love me. Emulate me. Because I deserve it. I did it all.

But, there are still a few people I would like to thank. Mostly because I am contractually bound to do so....

First and foremost, I would like to thank all the people at Finnean Nilsen Projects that made this dream of mine a reality. My tireless editor, Tom, who knocked me out at the Christmas party and turned my travesty of a first draft into the masterpiece you're about to read. My producer, Ryan, who really made this thing happen, put it all together, leant me his wife, and pushed this concept beyond anything I could have hoped for. Without you guys, this project would still be a fantasy.

To my girl ~~Sherry~~ Janet, for being there. Lying there, really. And, lastly, my parents, for kicking me out of the house and forcing me to earn my own money. Thanks to all. And no, I'm not buying any of you a fucking yacht.

Rick Glacier: PI
in

FIST FULL OF BRUNETTES

A Multiple-Choice Thriller
BY BILL PRYST

A Finnean Nilsen Project

A Ryan Lowenstein Production

A Thomas Sweeney Book

In Association with Swinging Dick Media

Starring Rick Glacier as Himself

Executive-Produced by Leila Morton

Director of Typography Wallace Lowenstein

Do you hate Hollywood as much as we do?

CHAPTER ONE

The whiskey was turning sour in my mouth. The book in my hands was boring me. I had been in that office for six weeks and no one had walked through the door. After five years on the force, taking down bootleggers and speak-easies, cracking heads on vice, catching eighteen murderers on my own, I thought my services would be in demand as a PI. Maybe it had been done. Maybe I was a cliché.

I set my dime novel on the table and sighed. I couldn't make rent. Ten bucks short. My bottle was almost empty. I'd have to dip into the rent money the fifty cents it would cost for a new one. If someone didn't walk in and offer me a job, right then, I was flat out on my ass.

Behind me, the city rolled by in a torrent of blaring horns and shouting tourists. Every building dripping with neon and flash bulbs. All dressed up with no place to go. Night brighter than the day. Big city life. It's a fun place to visit, but I didn't want to live here.

A quiet rapping on my glass door drew my attention. The silhouette through the frosted glass was vague, the eye in the center obscuring the form. It was either a job, or my landlord coming for the rent. He was early; it was only due two weeks ago.

"Yeah," I called and lit another smoke, the gentle puff swimming past me in the stagnant air. The knob turned and the door opened. In walked a knock-out. Long, curly blond hair. Pale skin. Good, full lips and a strong jaw. I like that in a woman. A strong jaw, that is. Her legs were longer than Pennsylvania Avenue, and her light satin dress clung to her curves like a child with separation anxiety. She had a small bag in one hand, a cigarette in a holder at her mouth.

"Mister Glacier?"

"That's me," I half-rose from my chair, picked the hat off my head and set it on the desk, out of respect. "Please, have a seat."

She crossed the room like an angel. Those long legs making her float rather than walk. Her eyes were light gray in the darkness of my office. I was betting they'd be florescent blue under the right circumstances.

"How can I help you?" I asked.

"You are *the* Rick Glacier, aren't you?"

"Do I look like a Rick Glacier to you?"

"You look big and cold," she said.

"Bingo, babe."

"But you're the private investigator."

It wasn't a question, but I answered it anyway.

"That's what it says on the door." I waved a palm at the frosted glass, pointed at the eye. "How can I help you?" I asked again.

"It's my husband." Her voice was soft, and the way she held her smoke made me think she was good with her hands, better with her lips. "He's been missing now for a week."

"Call the cops," I instructed. "That's what they're there for."

I watched her lips part as she touched them softly with the tip of the holder, then close around and pull some of the smoke in.

"I heard you used to be a cop," she said.

"Sure."

"And a war hero."

"That's the rumor."

"Well," she shrugged, "I'm calling you."

I sighed. She was too much to look at for too long. If I took the job, well, who knows what would happen with this dame.

"It's fifty dollars a day," I said, it was really twenty, but she looked like she had it, "plus expenses. And I take a retainer."

"How much is the retainer?"

I thought about it for a minute, weighing my options.

A. Tell her fifty bucks – flip to Chapter 2a.

B. Tell her twenty bucks – flip to Chapter 2b.

C. Tell her she's the retainer – flip to Chapter 2c.

CHAPTER 2A

"Fifty," I said, "first day's pay in advance."

"That seems reasonable." She opened her bag and pulled out a wad of cash. I had seen stacks like it on the force: bootlegger's money. Bankrolls. She tossed two twenties and a ten on my desk, and smiled at me. "Do you need some information?"

I shrugged.

"Sure I do. What's he look like? Got a picture?"

She produced one from her bag and slid it across my desk. The guy looked familiar, but I couldn't place him.

"He's one of Delaney's boys," she informed me. I nodded, that's where I knew the bastard from. "And now he's just suddenly gone. That's why I came to you. The cops just assume he's been taken out by his buddies."

"Or the competition."

"It wouldn't be them." She shook her head. "He's a banker. It wouldn't do them any good."

"What's a girl like you doin' married to a mob banker?" I asked before I thought it out. I have a tendency to do that at times. Sometimes it gets me into trouble. But it always gets me someplace. "I mean," I collected my thoughts; "I just thought you'd be an actress or singer or something."

She batted her lashes and smiled. "Well," she said, "I was an actress, actually, in the pictures. But when I met Sammy, I gave it up. He's very charming."

"I think I remember him now," I said. "He testified at Delaney's trial last year. Said all the taxes were in order."

"Right." She nodded this time, her hair staying perfectly styled. "Ever since then he's been on the payroll."

"Way I hear it: he was already on the payroll. That's why Delaney walked."

She shrugged. "There are a lot of rumors, Mister Glacier."

"Call me Rick." I looked at the picture again. "Or Glacier. I remember him as being a squirrelly little guy. Not what I would call charming."

"What's that got to do with anything?"

"Just trying to get a good picture," I explained. Really, I was probing to see how solid the marriage was. It wouldn't do me any good to come right out and ask, though. "You see, I need to get a full understanding of his life, his habits. It'll help when I'm trying to find him. That makes sense, doesn't it?"

"I guess." She nodded slowly. She was sizing me up for something and I didn't think it was a suit. "But let's keep away from the private things."

"Nothings private when a man's missing, Miss Marx...."

"Missus."

"Of course, Missus Marx. You can tell me what you want. But try to understand that the more you tell me, the easier it will be to find your husband."

"Call me Melanie," she said, and then squirmed for a moment. "Fine," she huffed, "he's not incredibly charming. He made me quit so other men couldn't look at me. He didn't approve of his wife being ogled by hundreds of men."

"Who could blame him?" I asked. All I wanted to do was look at her. She was like a shot of fire-water, seeing her woke up certain parts of me. I liked the feeling.

"But, he's a good man," she assured me. "He promised me he was going to get out of the business. He just wanted to be a banker, not a mobster."

"Do you love him?" Again I hadn't really thought that question out.

"Of course I love him," she gasped. "He's my husband."

"You wanna know how these things usually turn out?" I asked, didn't wait for an answer. "Usually it's the wife that does it. Or her boyfriend. I'm just being honest because I want us on the same page."

"That's fine," she sneered at me. "And I understand how these things work. I came to you for discretion."

Now we were getting someplace.

"What kind of discretion?"

She squirmed again. "I might be seeing someone."

"Who?"

"None of your business, that's who," she snarled, the smoke dangling daintily from between two fingers. I was liking the way she held it. Liking the way she pulled off it. By the way she flicked the end of the cigarette holder, I was certain she knew how to use that tongue of hers too.

"Listen lady, I need to know."

"Roger Delaney," she blurted. "We've been seeing each other for a few months now."

"Then why the hell are you here?" I asked. "I can't help you. You know what happened: Roger doesn't share his women. Your husband is in the Hudson, would be my guess."

"Don't say that."

"It's the truth."

"I don't love Roger." She shook her head. I could see a tear in the corner of her right eye. Seemed like a real one, and since I couldn't figure any other reason for her to be here, I'd say she really did love the banker. "He just... fulfills my needs."

"Hell, lady. There's a lot of guys that can do that. You don't need to see the King of New York for it."

"It's too late," she started to sob. "I've killed my husband!"

"Now, now. Come on." I rose from the desk and worked my way around to where she sat, weeping into her palms. I took the cigarette from between her fingers and stamped it out, pulling her close. Something about seeing a broad cry has never sat well with me. Instinct, I guess, because I've never been accused of being the chivalrous type.

"We don't know that." I did. "He could just be in hiding or something. Whatever happened to him, I'll get to the bottom of it. And if something bad happened, I'll get it fixed. You can count on me."

She shuddered.

"Thank you," she said, "you're a good man. I knew you could help me."

"In the meantime, you need a place to stay. Roger'll be looking for you. You have any family, friends he doesn't know about?"

"No, he knows everything." She shivered in my arms, the crystalline shadows playing along her body from the street lights.

"What about you?" I asked. "You know everything?"

"About you and Roger?"

"Yeah."

"I know he's not too fond of you." She smiled.

"You know I knocked his block off back in Sicily?"

"I know enough to know he can be very vengeful." She looked up at me with big, storming blue eyes. The realization that she was all mixed up with a man that could kill her and not lose a wink of sleep clouding the pupils. "What should I do?"

"Well," I shrugged, "you can stay at my place." I thought that one through completely. "It'll be no problem, and you'll be safe there."

"What about your wife?"

"Don't mention it."

I took her hands and pulled her out of the chair. Her skin was smooth and soft. I leaned forward and tested her response. She didn't back away. Our lips touched and I felt a jolt of electricity. She collapsed into my arms, and her tongue entered my mouth, rolling against mine, tasting me. Beyond the tobacco she tasted like grapes, probably wine, and a faint hint of strawberries.

Maybe I was taking advantage of her. She needed someone and I was ready and willing to be that someone, at least for the moment. In the morning, I had no idea how I would find her husband, but for the night, I was all the man she could handle.

We took a cab back to my place, and fell into each other's arms as soon as we crossed the threshold. My apartment's small, not much of a place for entertaining, but the largest room is the bedroom, which pretty much cuts out the fore-play and leads the babes where I want them.

She lost the dress, and I lost my pants. Not true, I knew where they were, I just didn't care. They lay beside her satin dress on the thin carpet.

Her body was warm and smooth. Her hips shaped per-fectly for the stroke of my palm. She lay on the bed and I helped her forget her husband. She tasted salty and fresh. I watched her face through the V of her thighs past her breasts, small and supple, slowly rising.

I bet she was one hell of an actress.

When she was done rubbing my hair and moaning, I let her spend some time on me. She was good, a real pro. She knew how to use the feminine weapons God had armed her with. Her full lips and talented tongue dangerously attentive to areas of my body that had already been primed and pumped by her slender fingers. It was everything I could do not to ruin the moment by arriving early.

The moon was silently watching through the window as she lay back on the bed. The thick blankets I use to shut out the New York winters splayed around her like the stuffing of the package from heaven she must have sprung from. Her long legs opened and her eyes told me she was ready.

I took her missionary. A little light for my tastes, but tried and true and it gave us plenty of face to face contact. Her lips were soft and welcoming. Her body young and virile. I pulled her into my arms and kissed her hard. She took it, and gently bit my lips with playful anticipation of the moment to come. Her breasts pressed flat against my chest, and I could feel her stomach muscles rolling as her hips rose and fell. I felt her lower abdomen spasm as she drew close to orgasm, and then she gripped me tight with her body, gasping. Finally her body relaxed.

But I wasn't finished yet.

I rolled her onto her stomach, wrapped my arm under her and pulled her ass up. She was a damn fine specimen. The arch of her back as it rose into the air and the apple-like shape of her buttocks made my mouth water. Her head fell back as I slowly entered her.

I took it slow, didn't want to hurt her. She fell into a trance as I began pumping, her light moans flowing together into one, breathless crescendo. I let her have it full inside her, forgot to pull out. She didn't seem to mind. I heard a soft giggle from the sheets where her face was buried, and then she rolled onto her back, gasping.

I flopped down beside her and sparked two butts, setting one gently between her lips. I didn't know where her holder was.

"Well, Mister Glacier," she said, "you certainly live up to your reputation."

"Thank you." I pulled the smoke deep into my lungs. I would need energy if I was going to keep this up all night. Which was likely. "Now, before we go again, I have some more questions."

(Continue on to Chapter 3)

CHAPTER 2B

"Well," I sighed, "usually it's fifty, the first day's in advance. But," I shrugged, looked at her through my eyebrows, "for you, I'll make it twenty."

"I would hate to think you were treating me differently than your other clients." She smiled with her eyes. The look in them said she wanted to be treated *very* differently than my other clients. I didn't have the heart to tell her she was my only client, so I let it slide. I didn't want her to stop looking at me like that, either. She sat up, as if sensing my thought, "Mister Glacier?"

"Yup," I tried to clear my head. She was like a mist, filling my brain. "Like I said, for you, twenty."

A smile flicked across her lips as she opened her bag and pulled out ten crisp two dollar bills and ticked them off onto the table like she was dealing a winning poker hand. I glanced at them. I had just made rent, but I had other things on my mind.

"So tell me about him." I left the money where she had dealt it and looked into the gray of her eyes. "Your husband."

She opened her bag again and produced a picture, which she laid beside the money. I rose from my chair just a hair, slid the picture over to my side of the desk and looked at it. I didn't like the face that stared back.

"Hell, kid, that's Sammy Marx," I told her. I figured she probably already knew. "He works for Roger Delaney."

She nodded, "Yes."

"You'll just have to take those deuces back. I can tell you right now where your husband is." I studied her for a moment, waiting for a flicker of comprehension, but it seemed to elude her. I told her, "He's at the bottom of the Hudson."

"Roger wouldn't get rid of him," she shook her head. "Sammy does all his financials."

"Well, even if he didn't, I can't help you. Me and Delaney don't exactly see eye to eye."

"I heard you punched him in Sicily."

"You heard right." I leaned back. "And he had it coming."

"Mister Glacier…"

"And don't forget about your husband," I stopped her. "He's the only reason Delaney walked on the tax beef. The feds send him up on the stand, and from what I hear it only took ten thousand to have him perjure himself so Delaney walks. Now he's on the payroll. I don't know if you know, babe, but I helped on that case."

"I wasn't aware," she said stiffly.

"So, honestly, I ain't real eager to find Mister Marx. I just don't see how it would benefit me, is what I'm saying."

"The money…"

"That's mob money," I scoffed. "It's not worth the paper it's printed on to me."

"Mister Glacier," she huffed, "I'm certain we can come to some type of arrangement."

"You think?"

She stood up and pressed her cigarette into my ashtray. The holder stayed attached to the butt, and she ignored it. I looked into her eyes as she sauntered around the desk and came up beside me. Her left hand dropped the bag onto my desk, her right slid along my arm, up to my chest.

"A man like you," she said softly into my ear. I felt her breath, hot and moist against my neck, "can get whatever he wants."

"Yeah," I grunted. "I take what I want, alright."

"So take it."

"I want you," I said. The truth of that statement strained against my zipper.

She stood up very straight and brushed her hair back.

"Mister Glacier, I am a respectable woman. I will not be spoken to in that manner."

So that's how she wanted to play it? I could do it her way. I stood from my chair, my face very close to hers. She took a step back and I slapped her hard across the mouth, snapping her head to the side.

"Babe," I said, "where I come from, a woman does what she's told."

I saw blood rush to her face, my hand print a scarlet stain across her cheek. Her eyes turned a bright, burning blue, chest rapidly rising and falling. If I looked hard enough, I could have seen her pulse in her throat. I wasn't looking at her throat.

I stepped forward and kissed her hard on the lips. She pulled away, but I caught her. Her muscles tensed as my tongue plunged into her mouth. She struggled for a moment before surrendering, her tongue performing an erotic tango with mine.

My hands slid down her thighs, yanking her skirt up, waist high. I probed between her legs and found no cloth, just smooth moist skin and soft hair. She pulled her lips from me, gasping for air.

"You want it on the desk?" I asked.

"Mister Glacier," she chastised, "I'm not paying you to talk."

I swiped my arm across the desk, sending papers, ashtrays and her bag to the floor. I spun and threw her onto it. She slid her hands into the top of her dress and spilled out two small, supple breasts. Her ragged moans vibrated in my ears as I suckled first one breast and then the other, the small nipples beading when I teased them with my lips. She squealed when I nipped at them and pushed me away, spreading her legs wider to give me a glimpse of the juices shimmering on her thighs.

I entered her roughly, groaning as I sank into her. Her hands came up and curled into fists, hammering blows to my chest before her perfectly manicured nails raked a painful path across my pectorals. I roared and dug my fingers into the supple flesh of her ass, groaning again when those long legs of hers anchored around my hips, pulling me in as deep as I could go.

I drilled her hard, so hard I thought I might be bruising her thighs. If I *was* bruising her, she obviously considered it a pleasurable pain because her wild moans escalated into a high pitched howl of ecstasy. At least that's what I assumed she was screaming about until I realized it wasn't my name she was calling.

"Rape!" she screamed. "Rape! He's raping me!"

The nice thing about New York is: you can scream just about anything and people will ignore you. So long as you don't scream "fire!" nobody will give a damn. It helps if you're not moaning it, as well. I kept on pummeling her thighs until she gasped for breath and went rigid.

"Oh…My…God!" she moaned, as I pulled out and flipped her around so her ass was nestled against my thighs

"Okay," I growled, "enough fun for you." I grabbed a fistful of her hair and pulled. She yelped in pain, or pleasure, I couldn't tell and didn't care anymore. Then I slammed myself back inside her and rammed as hard as I could. I kept up a frantic pace, certain I was hurting her, and damn sure she was enjoying it. She was bent at the waist over my desk, her head cocked upward, staring at the ceiling as I pulled her long, blonde hair. Her breasts sliding along the smooth tabletop with each brutal thrust.

I felt her come, the rush of sweet smelling fluids urging me to follow her. I shoved into her hard and deep, holding myself rigid as an explosion of liquid heat shot up inside of her, then slowly ground my hips until I'd filled her completely, milking every last ounce of pleasure before pulling out. I left her there, her breath shallow but steady, and fell back into my chair and fumbled for a smoke.

"Damn right we can work something out," I mumbled as I flicked open my lighter and sparked it. "That's what we call 'aggressive negotiations,' babe."

Face down on the desk, her giggle was muffled.

"So," she tilted her head back to look at me, but kept her body draped across my desk, her ass still available if I wanted another go. "Does that mean you'll take the case?"

"Yeah," I blew smoke into her face, "and you'd better stay at my place for safekeeping. But just keep your ass like that. I have a few questions, and then I'll be ready for more negotiating."

(Continue on to Chapter 3)

CHAPTER 2C

"*You're* the retainer," I said. At that point, it was worth a shot. If I couldn't make rent, I could live with it, but I couldn't look myself in the mirror if I passed up an opportunity like this. "And I'll drop the price to twenty."

She blinked.

"Who do you think I am?" she demanded, her tone said she wasn't going to take the deal. Didn't blame her. She seemed like a classy broad. "You're disgusting! No wonder they kicked you off the force!"

She picked up my ash tray and dumped it on my head. Turned on her tall high-heels and walked out of my office. Out of my life. She took her ass, her legs, her sweet little tits and any chance of a paying job with her.

"Nice job, Glacier," I said. "Looks like the soup kitchen for you."

(That's right, bitch, you lost. That was fast, too. This is a classy dame. You can't talk to her like that. Of course, that's probably why you're reading this book and not knocking boots with a hottie. Look at yourself! Jesus! Go back to Chapter 1 and pick again, and have a little dignity this time. Women deserve respect, prick.)

CHAPTER 3

The next morning Mrs. Marx was gone, but I found a note in the kitchen saying she would meet me at an Italian joint downtown for dinner at seven. She left a lipstick imprint of her kiss at the bottom of the paper. I don't know why broads always feel the need to do things like that, they make me feel funny. I had a good time with the dame, but that didn't mean we were going steady.

I decided to fry up a pound of bacon and a half dozen eggs and spent an hour smoking, drinking coffee, and soaking up the bacon fat and egg yolks with white bread, thinking about where to begin. I knew Delaney owned a little dive in Brooklyn where he ran numbers. It was the only place in town that charged a buck for a sandwich, but I had a hunch that Sammy would have been a regular there. Most of Delaney's action took place between its walls, and Marx would need to be around to keep it all accounted in his neat little books.

I took a hack to the subway and the train to Brooklyn, walked the rest of the way from there for the exercise. The place was called "The Joint" for some reason, and on a Tuesday morning it was filled entirely with thick Italian street guys, sitting around drinking espresso and talking about the races. The bartender-slash-cook was a meaty bastard named Mike who never liked me much. But we served together on the eastern front and I killed enough Nazi's with him that he never gave me a hard time. Plus he loved my Luger, and made me tell the story of how I got it every time I saw him.

"Just one more time, Glacier," he said, his words gurgling past the fat in his throat. "How'd you take out the Kraut?"

"He was an officer," I said, the other guys at the bar didn't seem interested, but Mike was all ears, "and he was sitting at a table in Blintz, eating a Bratwurst. I came into the house with my Browning. He shouted something in German that they later explained meant 'I surrender' and I just opened up on him. Cut the guy damn near in half, right up from stem to sternum. And when I walked over to him, still sitting neatly next to his plate, was this sexy little pistol."

I laid it on the counter so Mike could examine it again. Somehow the flabby bastard had made it through the whole war without a single Luger. I knew guys that had dozens of them. One Corporal had so many he couldn't fit them all in his bag. But Mike didn't have a single thing to show for his time in Europe, save for his belly, which had started flat when he enlisted, and grown ever since VE day.

"Beautiful weapon." He nodded.

"Yup," I said, "the nine millimeter doesn't put 'em down like the forty-five, but if I put two or three in ya, you'll be dead just the same."

"Well, thanks for tellin' me the story again," Mike grumbled through his mucus. "But, that's not why you came down. What'ya need?"

"Just got some questions. Looking for someone."

"You know nobody around here is gonna talk to you, bub. It's a waste of time."

"I'm looking for Sammy Marx. His wife says he hasn't been home in a while."

Mike leaned back and nodded. He sized me up, as if he hadn't seen me before, and then flicked his gaze across the room.

"See those broads over there." He motioned with his big, jowly face. "They're in here all the time. Marx had his way with 'em all the time. They're here to service the boys, got me?"

"Yup."

"Maybe they could tell you where else he hangs out." He shrugged. "That's about all the help I can give you. And it's only on account of you showing that pretty little pistol of yours."

"Thanks Mike."

"Don't mention it." He leaned across the bar. "I mean that, don't tell nobody I told you nuthin."

"Understood."

I turned from the bar and saw three dames sitting in a booth, whispering to each other. As I approached, the chatter stopped and they each glared at me. To the left was a red headed thing of maybe ninety pounds; her skin light and freckled. She had blazing green eyes, and full soft lips that made me want to lick them. Center was brown haired with baby fat and what looked to be nice, full curves. Just enough meat on her to have some real fun with. Her nose was thin and slightly upturned, with high cheek bones and good skin. To the right was an older chick with black hair, going gray at the roots. She had the signs of wear all over her, wine tracks on her cheeks, crow's feet along her eyes, and tobacco stained teeth.

"I need to ask you kids some questions," I said. "But I think we might want some privacy to do it. Who wants to go first?"

"Well," the old broad said, "why don't you pick. Since you're such a big cop man, with the gun and all."

I glanced from one woman to the next, trying to decide who would break first, and who I shouldn't waste my time with.

A. The red head – flip to Chapter 4a.

B. The brunette – flip to Chapter 4b.

C. The old bird – flip to Chapter 4c.

CHAPTER 4A

"You," I told the red head, "let's go in the back and talk."

She slid out of the booth and followed me to the bathrooms. They would never let me in the back, where the money changed hands and the bets were jotted down, but the bathroom was quiet enough and gave us plenty of room. One thing that having a bunch of former soldiers for gangsters gave you was clean latrines.

I locked the door behind us, motioned for her to take a spot against the sinks, and leaned against the door. She wasn't a bad looking skirt when she was standing. She wore a flower dress. Her legs were short but smooth and freshly shaved. I could smell her perfume from across the room.

"I'm looking for Sammy Marx," I told her.

"So?"

"So, I heard maybe you know where he hangs."

"Sorry, fella, I don't know nuthin."

"Listen, babe, you'll tell me or I'll have to beat it outta ya."

"Go ahead and try." She laughed. "Your little prick can't hurt me. I'm used to real men."

I crossed the room and slapped her hard. She barely flinched. I looked down at her and smiled. She was a tough cookie. But I had ways to break even the worst girls. My hands went to her shoulders and I pushed her down. Then I pulled it out and let her get a look at it.

"Bigger than that?" I asked.

"No," she said softly, staring at it.

"Good. Because I'm going to break you like a damned horse."

I pulled her up and turned her around. Pressing her face into the wall, I pulled up her skirt and ripped her panties. She had a nice, small ass, but with enough meat to cushion the blows. I smacked it once, hard enough to bring a yelp, and then shoved my hand in front of her face.

"Lick it," I told her, my voice low, breath coming through forced.

She did as she was told. With a thick tongue that left enough saliva on my palm to get me started. I rubbed it on the head of my member to get it slick, and then pushed it into her ass. She was tight, never had a man inside that hole, and she screamed.

I heard someone beating on the door, but the lock held. I forced myself all the way in, and then pulled out. I felt her go limp as I did, but then I put it back right away, not waiting for her ass to close back up. I pounded her swollen hole, ramming myself in until I felt too much resistance. She was fighting but not getting away. Tears rolled down her cheeks.

"Where's he hang out?" I asked through heaving breathes. "Where?"

"Please..." she moaned. She could fight it all she wanted, but nature was taking its course and she was starting to enjoy it. "Please...."

I pulled out and let her sag to the floor. With my right hand I grabbed her chin and made her look at me.

"Now, tell me or I put this in your mouth."

She looked down at my manhood and shuddered.

"Please."

"Tell me!"

"At the Roxy," she mumbled. "On fifth."

"Good girl," I said. "Give me a name."

"A name?"

"Someone for me to talk to when I get there."

"Maxie," she moaned, "she's one of his girls."

I pulled her back up, turned her around and entered her ass again. She moaned. I thrust until I felt myself about to erupt, then I pulled out and sprayed across her ass, the back of her dress, and a few drops in her hair.

I left her in a heap on the floor, reached into my pocket and pulled out ten greenbacks and dropped them like confetti on the floor next to her. When I opened the door, Mike was standing in the doorway, looking foul.

"What the hell happened?"

"I asked her some questions."

"And?"

"I got what I came for."

(Continue to Chapter 5)

CHAPTER 4B

"You," I said to the brunette. "Let's talk outside."

The red haired dame slid out of the booth to allow her friend to pass. I led the girl outside, and in the light, she was beautiful. Full, shapely, and firm, she wore a pleated red dress and sandals. Her legs were thick but smooth, and her hair lay lightly against her cheeks. I wanted to roll around in the sheets for a few hours next to that body.

"I'm looking for…"

"Hey!" I heard a voice to my left that was familiar. "Hey, Rick Glacier. I never thought I'd see the day."

I turned to see Roger Delaney approaching with two goons. He flashed me a smile, but I felt the hairs on the back of my neck spring to life. Roger smiled like that when he smelled blood.

"I think I still owe you one, partner, for that business in Sicily." I saw the flash of a switchblade, but before I could reach my Luger he had buried the six inch blade in my liver. "That's for being a stand-up guy," he whispered.

I felt my knees go weak and slid to the ground. I could feel the poisonous bile from my organ seeping into my bloodstream. Roger stepped over me and approached the broad.

He questioned her for a moment and then slapped her one good. With his hand on her elbow, he ushered her inside. One of his men spat on me before he entered the bar. I felt a weight on my chest, and closed my eyes to rest.

(Nice job, douche bag, you got Rick smoked on his first real day on the job. You're a real ace at this, aren't you pal? Two pieces of advice: one, don't ever become a private investigator. With your instincts you'll be taking the long nap before noon your first day, just like Glacier. Two, go back to chapter three and pick again, and this time try to stay alive. Jack-ass.)

CHAPTER 4C

"You," I told the old broad. "Let's take a walk."

She slid out of the booth and followed me outside. I turned and started in the direction of the trains. She was older than I thought. Her hair was probably completely gray. She was just dying it with something powerful and hadn't made it back to the beautician lately. I told her to pick up the pace and she fell in beside me. I lit her a smoke and one for myself, then started asking questions.

"I'm looking for Sammy Marx," I told her. "I hear you might know where he likes to hang."

"Nope," she shook her head, "I'm too old for his likings. The boys just keep me around to run errands."

"But you must've heard him talking. The man ain't been home for a week. His wife is worried sick."

She glanced over at me, and then ran her gaze from my toes to my hairline. There was something in her eyes that said she wasn't past her old ways yet. They may only use her for errands, but she would've loved to still be in line for something rough.

"Maybe I heard something," she said finally. "I hear he likes to hang down at the Roxy. Got a couple of girls there he likes, and he likes showin' off his other girls there, too. For a banker he sure took to gangster life quick."

"The Roxy?" I asked. "That's the place down on fifth, right?"

"Yup." She took a long pull on her smoke. "But that ain't free. No way. Delaney would have me fish bait just for talking to you."

"True." I nodded. "But no one can hear what we're saying, babe. And Mike won't tell. He'd be in a world of hurt if Delaney knew he even let me in the bar."

She nodded, as much to herself as to me. We passed an alley and she stopped, looked down it and then turned to me. That fire I had seen before was back and blazing white hot.

"I want something for my trouble," she said.

"Okay."

"Not money, the boys keep me with plenty of money."

"I'm sure that's real nice, sugar, but the name of one club ain't exactly worth the rent." I tossed my Lucky Strike onto the sidewalk, grabbed a hold of her elbow and pulled her along.

"Now, I want more information, and you want something from me." I shrugged, looked down her shirt. I was surprised by how smooth the flesh of her cleavage was. Perhaps the parts I couldn't see weren't as damaged as the face was. I doubted it. "So let's say we go someplace we can talk more privately."

"Your place," she suggested.

"No," I laughed, "I might have a dame at my place."

"Might?"

"Yeah," I shrugged, "she might've come back." I caught her eyeballing me. "It's not like that, she's a client. I just can't have crazy old broads like you dancing around naked in front of clients. You know?"

"Who said I would be naked?"

"I did, babe. And that part isn't up for discussion. I don't trust women who're dressed."

She laughed and eyed me again. I kept my fingers between the flesh and bone of her left arm, and dug my fingertips a little deeper, turning her giggling into a squeal. She pawed at me but I didn't let go.

I hailed a cab and told him the address to a little hotel where I like to retire when I'm too far into the bottle to be seen in public. The cabby pulled the flag and we started moving. It was a long ways for a cab ride; the fare passed two dollars by the time he pulled to the curb. I looked over at the old dame, motioned for her to pay the man.

"What kind of a man are you?" she snapped.

"You said the boys kept you well fed," I said. "Pay the man, and I'll take care of you later."

"Take care of me how?" She didn't say it in a cutesy way, so I raised the back and of my hand to remind her of the various different scenarios that could play out inside the room.

"Fine, bub," she grumbled, "but you bruise me up and you'll have to answer to Mike. We've been more than jus' friends lately, and he won't see too kindly to a man like you roughing me up."

"Less talking, kid, more cash."

She handed me two singles from a stack of about twenty, I pulled an extra two from it and smiled my roughest grin at her. The cabby nodded as I passed them over, and I reminded him that it wasn't a good idea to tell anyone who was in his cab, or where he drove them. He nodded again and disappeared before I could fully close the door behind me.

The Huruba Hotel was about four cents short of being a one nickel dive, but the clientele was equally shady so the management didn't ask questions. They also charged by the hour, which I've always found useful when you can't imagine having to look at the dame for more than five minutes after you've pulled out of her.

The owner was a Jap who had used his time in internment to swindle his fellow "neighbors" out of whatever life savings Roosevelt hadn't confiscated. The second he was released he moved out to the Empire City and bought his own little slice of paradise, which he then began renting out at fifty-cents an hour to whores and their Johns.

I tossed the guy one of the gal's singles and got a ticket for room twenty in return.

"What's your name, kid?" I asked. It was getting increasingly difficult to refer to her as "the old broad" in my head. Not that I cared what her name was, I just thought it might get in the way if I had to say, "take it old broad! You like that don't ya, you old skirt!"

"Deborah."

"Ok, Deb." I nodded. She followed me to the self-serve elevator, and we walked from there to room twenty, where I unlocked the door and pushed her in. The room was small, just a bed and end table, a radio and a bathroom. "Take a shower, Deb. I don't touch half-clean broads."

"You're such a romantic," she said, dryly. "I can see why the girls throw themselves at you."

"And make it snappy." I lit a Lucky and tossed my lighter on the bed. "I want my questions answered before we get to the fun part."

She took a shower, if a three minute sprint through running water could be called that, and when she came back out she looked damn fine for a woman well past her prime. She had one of the rough towels wrapped around her waist, another around her hair, and nothing across her chest. Her breasts were large but firm, surprising for her age, and they had nipples that jutted out, begging to be nibbled on.

"So, the Roxy," I said as way of greeting. "How often does he hang there?"

"Almost every night." She rubbed her hair with the towel. "Like I said, if he's single for the night he picks up girls there, if he's got a looker he brings 'em there to show off."

"So that's it? That's his only spot?"

"He hits the Trio Club up town, too. Where the rest of the bankers drink. I guess he likes to feel like he's still legit, at some point."

"When's the last time you saw him?"

She thought for a minute. "Five days ago."

"Wife hasn't seen him in a week."

"Mister, it wouldn't be the first time a man saw me 'stead of seeing his wife, probably won't be the last."

"You said you were too old for him."

"I am."

"So?"

She sighed. "Last time I seen him he was hitting the bottle pretty hard. His hands were shaking like flags in a hard breeze. The other girls had gone home, and he was the last of the boys at the bar. Mike left us there and told Sammy to lock up. We got to talking and one thing led to another."

"I see." I took a good, long look at her tits. Her face looked fifty but her bosoms looked under thirty. I wondered how she pulled it off. I'd heard of doctors who could cut a babe's breast open and put bags of salt water in them, but

I couldn't imagine they looked that good, and they weren't exactly legal yet, either. "What did you talk about?"

"Oh." She shrugged, dropped the towel from her hair and rocked her head back and forth, fluffing the old curls with the dry, stale air of the hotel room. "This and that."

"Was he worried about anything?" I asked, finally looked up into her face. "Afraid of anybody?"

"Not that he spoke of." She crossed the room to where I sat on the ruffled mattress. I watched her hands trace up along her hips, and then her fingertips explored the thin skin and muscles of her stomach. She moved them up into the canyon between her large breasts, and let her palms fall over her nipples. "Any more questions?"

"Lots."

"Can they wait?" She slid her left hand down and undid the towel, letting it drop to the floor in a damp heap around her ankles. "For a little while."

"Babe," I said, and my breath caught deep in my throat. Her bottom half looked as young as her chest. I figured it was the smoking and drinking and hard life that ran her face into the ground. Probably years of beatings and the stress of mob life, and being a possession of a bunch of classless men that turned her hair. But somewhere in there, there was still a girl who loved a good, rough time in the sack. I thought I'd like to see that girl again. "I don't remember what the questions were."

She knelt down and sidled her way between my legs. Her lips were swollen, as if she'd licked them continuously in preparation for a meal. She wore no cosmetics, and it actually made her look younger. The crow's feet were gone, though the wine lines were more pronounced. She slid her long fingers over the bulge in my pants, and rubbed it for a moment.

She gazed into my eyes. "I look alright down here?"

"Kid," I leaned forward and took her by the shoulders, "you look just fine." I took her by the hair and pressed her face into my groin. I hadn't even felt my penis freed from the restrictions of my clothing before I felt a wet, hot mouth wrap around the head and slide down the shaft.

I felt her tonsils rubbing against the sensitive tip, and her tongue pressed me into her cheek. Her left palm rubbed my balls as the right slid its way along the fibers of my pants. She took as much of me in her mouth as she could, slurping as she pulled all fourteen inches back out. I looked down into her eyes as she wiped drool from her chin.

"I need a name," I said softly. "One of his girls I can talk to at the Roxy."

"Maxie." Her voice was a low growl. "Now give me what I want."

"Dames don't order me around."

"Well, Mister Glacier," she taunted, "what are you gonna do about it?"

I pulled her up onto the bed and rolled on top of her. Her hands flailed and I caught them by the wrists, using my knees to pin them down to the thin mattress. Then I leaned over and kissed her aged lips, swollen from fellatio.

I felt her tongue move inside my mouth, and she curled it around my own and pulled it between her lips. She used her lips like a vacuum, sucking my tongue into her throat, sliding it in and out, her lips playing with it like she had my phallus. When she finally released me, I reared back, my knees still trapping her wrists against the mattress.

"I like to gag," she muttered. "I like it all the way in my throat. That's how I want to be paid. Gag me."

I touched her cheek and rubbed it. She was truly beautiful in her way. I used three fingers to open her mouth, sliding them down her throat as far as they would go. When I pulled them out she smiled back at me.

"You sure about this, babe?"

"Nope."

I leaned forward and guided my erection between her waiting lips. I inched myself in further, until I felt her stiffen, her hands wiggling and her fingers curved. Her eyes widened, and then she nodded, slightly, as much as she could with her throat stuffed with my engorged flesh. I sank deeper, until the constriction of her larynx would allow me no further, and then began slow, methodical strokes.

I gave four long strokes before she began writhing. I pulled out and she coughed violently, a small river of saliva, thick as mucus, pouring out from her lips.

"Again," she gasped, "and deeper this time."

"Darling," I grinned, "I do believe I'm in love with you."

This time I showed no mercy. I jammed my member into her throat until her eyes rolled back and she started to go limp. When I pulled out she gasped and coughed, then laughed, and chased the tip of my penis with her mouth.

"More, dammit," she moaned, "more please."

"Alright, Miss Twist."

I gave it to her three more times, until her eyes were swollen from the exertion and her throat was so course she croaked when she tried to talk. I could feel my balls swelling with anticipation. Her firm breasts, thin neck, soft, clean cheeks, all coated with thick, slimy spit and she licked the corners of her mouth to clean it off. I held her down, but relented for a moment to give her enough room to run her thick tongue between her breasts.

"Now my tits," she croaked. "Make love to my tits and let me have all your cum on my face." She smiled. "Try to get as much as you can in my mouth, though."

I leaned back, pressed her breasts together with my hands and slid my manhood between them. The flesh was smooth and soft and supple, molding itself around my veined shaft. I pumped for five minutes, until I felt the surge overcoming me. She kept her mouth open just enough for my tip to slip between her lips each time my rod was fully engulfed by her bosom. When the helmet would slide into her mouth she would flick the most sensitive points with her tongue playfully.

"Give it to me, Glacier," she growled, "I want it, now!"

"No dame orders me around!"

I moaned, and then felt myself boil over, covering her face, breasts and mouth with eight full shots. She licked her lips, and when I released some pressure on her limbs she shot forward to suck my sperm from her tits. I stood and set her free. She used her hands to clean her face, and then licked them clean. At that moment, she was simultaneously the most disturbing and sexy sight I had ever seen.

I sparked a smoke and laid it between her inflamed lips.

"Well, Deb."

"I like Debby better."

"Okay, Debby." I nodded, tried to catch my breath. "I'll tell you what. Anytime you want to get together and have a little fun, you just call me." I handed her a card.

"Are you gonna give me a lift back to the Joint?"

"No, kid, I got things to do." I pulled my pants back on and smiled at her. "Here," I tossed her my pack of smokes, then dug in my pocket, pulled out a ten and laid it atop the Lucky's, "that'll get you home."

"Thank you, Mister Glacier," she called as I reached the door.

"For what?"

"For making me feel special again." She had a tear in her right eye, I didn't know if it was from the asphyxiation or real emotion.

"Dames," I grumbled as I closed the door behind me, "they're all as nutty as a can of Planters."

(Continue to Chapter 5)

CHAPTER 5

I decided to head back to the office and get the paperwork moving on the Marx case before hitting the Roxy. It wouldn't do any good to be there before five, as the doors would be locked up tight and it would be completely empty, save for maybe a few wise-guys playing cards on the top floor. The bartender would be in about five-fifteen, and I would be waiting for him. That was my plan.

As I walked into my office I saw something that both repelled me and made me smile. Carlene, the landlord's twenty-two year old daughter, was standing in the middle of the floor, mopping the asbestos. She was repellant in that I still owed rent, and though I had it to give, thanks to the retainer Mrs. Marx had paid me; I didn't really want to part with it if I didn't have to.

But, she also made me smile.

She made me smile because she was twenty-two and single. She had short sand-colored hair that curled into a bob. Her skin was deeply tanned from weekends at the Jersey Shore. She wore a light, flower patterned dress that ended just below the knees with eloquently braided lines of lace. Her hips were thin but well rounded, and even through the fabric of her gown her pert little breasts were evident.

"Mister Glacier," she sighed when she saw me walk in, "my Poppa was hoping I'd catch you here."

"Good morning to you, too, Carlene. You know, when are you going to take me up for dinner?"

"When you have the money to pay my old man," she smiled wryly, "and the restaurant bill."

"Well," I smirked, "that just may be today."

I pulled a hundred bucks from my pocket, rolled up into a tight cylinder and wrapped with a rubber band. I tossed it to her and she caught it with both hands.

"All here?" she asked with a raised eyebrow.

"Yes ma'am." I nodded. "One hundred."

"Well, I'll be. We never thought you'd come up with it, after all."

"Neither did I," I said honestly, another one of those times I didn't think it through. "But I got a good job yesterday. In fact, that's why I asked about dinner. I need to go to the Roxy tonight, ask some questions. I wouldn't mind having a classy babe like you on my arm."

"Well, well, Mister Glacier," she smiled, shifting her body weight from one hip to the other, "I do believe that's the nicest thing you've ever said to me."

"I certainly hope not."

From behind me I heard wooded soles slapping hard and fast as they moved down the hall. I turned just in time to see Harmon Phelps walk through my open office door. He was watching his shoes as he walked and almost ran right into me. Harmon's a full six inches shorter than me, so I was able to avoid the collision by reaching out and pressing my palm to his forehead as he made the turn from hall to threshold. I glanced down and noticed his shoes were new. He must have been admiring them as he walked.

"Mister Phelps." I nodded.

"Mister Glacier," he shook his head, "I don't suppose you have any money for me? Hmm?"

"Actually Poppa," Carlene tossed him the roll, "he's got it."

"All here?" He glared at me, his right eye was bigger than his left, making it appear as if a magnifier was placed over it.

"Why does everyone keep asking me that?" I held up my hands in defense. "Do I look like a man who can't count?"

"You look like a man who'd do anything to shirk his responsibilities," Harmon growled. "You know, there's a two dollar fine for being late. I should make you pay that. I have bills too, you know."

"Poppa," Carlene sighed, "Rick was just telling me about a job he got."

"Job?"

"An investigation," I explained.

"And he invited me out to dinner tonight," she blushed, "as a kind of chaperone. To the Roxy."

"The Roxy?" Harmon frowned. "Ain't that a mob joint?"

"Just a rumor." I shrugged. "It's actually a pretty classy place. Anyway, the guy I'm looking for is a regular there. His wife is worried sick about him."

"Not going to happen," Harmon announced. "No daughter of mine is going to a gangster hang-out with the likes of you."

"I'm going to ignore the insult," I growled, "out of respect for your daughter."

"Poppa," Carlene's voice was low and firm. "I am a grown woman now, and I will accompany any man I see fit, anywhere I see fit."

"Not so long as you're my daughter, and living in my house."

"That's fine," she shrugged, "we'll just see what Mamma has to say about it." She stormed out of the room, leaving the mop bucket and a large pool of water on the floor in the middle of my office.

"Don't bring your mother into it." Harmon chased her. "It'll just make my life hell."

Carlene's head popped back through the doorway. "What time are you picking me up?" she asked playfully.

I thought for a moment.

A. Tell her four-thirty at the office – flip to Chapter 6a.

B. Tell her seven at the office – flip to Chapter 6b.

C. Tell her eight at your place – flip to Chapter 6c.

CHAPTER 6A

"Meet me here at four-thirty," I told her, "I've got a seven o'clock with my client. That way we can get some answers before I meet up with her, and maybe take in a picture afterward."

"Let's take it one thing at a time." She winked. "See ya at four-thirty."

I left the mop, the puddle, and the office exactly how I'd found it and made my way home. I had a few hours to kill before I had to meet up with Carlene and I figured it would be good to wash the last broad off me before I spent any real quality time with the landlord's baby girl.

As I soaked beneath the scalding water, I had two things on my mind. First off, I had to come to grips with the fact that the day had thus far been mostly a waste. Other than getting my rocks off and getting a single name at a single club, I hadn't really accomplished much. A date with Carlene was a great thing. That girl had made my balls itch and my brow break out in sweat since the first time we met. But it didn't help the case, not one bit.

Beyond that, I was flat broke. Again. Between the dame and the rent, I was out my savings and my retainer. Technically, I could hit up Mrs. Marx for today's wage, but I wasn't due to meet with her until seven and my date was at four-thirty. I also wasn't sure how she would react if I found her and asked for money to take out another skirt. After the romp last evening, and the kiss-signature on her note that morning, it was hard to say exactly how she saw our relationship. I thought it was pretty safe to say she felt like more than a client.

I stepped out of the shower and toweled off, utterly at a loss for my next move. I spent the next half-hour sitting naked at my kitchen table cleaning my Luger. The simplicity of the weapon always helped clear my mind. Where could I get some cash? Mrs. Marx. She was pretty much my only chance. I didn't have to tell her I was bringing company to the Roxy. It was obvious that I couldn't bring her to the club. Delaney would turn murderous if he saw me and that dame together. More murderous than usual, anyway.

But where did I find her?

There was a knock at my door and I took a moment to put my heater back together before I answered. I slid the clip in, pulled back the slide and released it, loading a round into the chamber.

I didn't take a moment to get dressed.

Mrs. Marx seemed impressed when she looked me up and down, a devilish smirk on her lips.

"Well, well, Mister Glacier," she said, "were you expecting me?"

"No, ma'am." I shook my head slowly. "But I am glad to see you."

"Is that so?" She pressed past me and entered the kitchen, dropping a bag of clothes on the table. She didn't bother to move my brushes and oils out of the way, so I figured at least a piece or two of her new clothing would be ruined by the grease.

"I need my pay."

"Pay?" She fluttered her eyelashes in confusion. "I paid you your advance last night."

"I need my day's pay," I told her, laid my Luger on the table and pulled her close, so that my growing erection could be felt through her thin skirt. "I had to purchase some information today, pay for cabs, and pay my rent, I'm tapped out."

She pushed herself away from me, lit a smoke, tossed the pack and a book of matches on the counter and then sat at the table. "Information? What did you hear?"

"Your husband hangs at a place called the Roxy. It's an upscale joint down on fifth. He ever take you there?"

"No."

"Well, apparently he took his other girls there. I guess he had some babes where he worked as well. I'll be heading to the club in a bit to see if I can't get more information."

"And it costs money to get this information?"

"Everything costs money, Missus Marx."

"Melanie."

"Right."

"Fine," she sighed, "why don't I just pay you for today and tomorrow? That way we won't have to worry about you running low."

"Remember," I said, standing two feet in front of her, my erection throbbing at about eye level, "it's fifty plus expenses."

"How much have you spent today?" she asked.

I thought about tossing ten dollars to a broad, decided not to mention it. "Don't worry about today's expenses," I said. "I forgot to get receipts. We'll start with the expense report tonight."

"That's fine." She nodded, her eyes locked on my manhood. She slipped a dainty hand into her bag and pulled out two fifty-dollar bills, laid them on the table neatly. "Will that hold you over?"

I looked down at the bills. I couldn't remember the last time I saw a fifty, must've been on vise. Gangsters were just about the only people with that had kind of loot. I picked them up and moved across the kitchen, depositing them into the pocket of the pants that were hanging off the knob of a cupboard.

"Well," I sighed, "I guess I had better get dressed."

"Why?" She batted her lashes again. I could see hunger in her eyes. "What time were you planning on heading to the Roxy?"

"Four-thirty," I told her. I didn't make a move to pull my pants from the knob. "The bartender should be there about five, which means I'll catch him just as he's coming in. I'll have his undivided attention."

"Should I come with you?"

"No way, babe. Delaney might be there…"

"He doesn't own the Roxy, does he?"

"Not that I know of," I shrugged, hadn't thought about it, "but if Sammy likes it there, odds are that Roger does too. Roger's not big on letting his boys hang in places he doesn't control."

"True," she agreed. Her hungry eyes didn't leave my waist. "Are you nervous?"

"Why would I be?"

"You answered the door with your pistol."

"I always do."

"I just thought," she paused, a coy smile playing around the corners of her mouth, "well, maybe you're not quite *ready* for all this mob stuff."

"Watch that smart mouth of yours, babe," I warned. "It won't get you nowhere good talking to me like that."

"You watch it," she said. She rose from her chair and crossed the room, stopped an inch from my face, tilting her head back so she could look into my eyes. She smiled as her long, smooth fingers wrapped around my manhood. "Just watch what it can do."

She dropped to her knees and engulfed my member, shoving it into her throat like it would save her life. She sucked it in hard, rolling her tongue over the tip and playfully slurping it from side to side. I braced my arms against my kitchen sink to keep my knees from buckling and leaned back, letting her do her thing. She sucked it down three times, then pulled it out and stroked the shaft for a few moments with her hand.

I looked down at her and she gazed up through big, blue eyes and giggled. She was a real shark. I fished to my left and found her pack of Lucky's and a book of matches. I struck a match and sent the end of the Lucky into embers, the epitome of nonchalance as I watched her work.

She had a lot of talent. Her mouth looked as good with me inside it as I felt being there. She kept pressure on with her tongue as she stroked the bottom of the shaft with three fingers, her left hand cradling my moist balls, rolling them like dice. All the while she bored into me with those stormy blues of hers. My mind started drifting as I felt fluid rise up from my nuts and fill the rest of me. What was her game? I looked at the book of matches in my hand, and tossed them back on the counter.

I heard her moan a bit in delight as I filled her mouth with my seed. When I was done, she slid back onto her ass on the floor, and I let my arms take all my weight as I leaned there, shivering.

"Good?" she asked, wiped a drop of silver from her lip with a finger and then popped it into her mouth.

"Just fine," I sighed. "You're a very talented woman."

She checked her watched and laughed. "You had better get a move on, Mister Glacier. It's four-fifteen."

I dropped my smoke in the sink, pulled on my clothes and gave her a peck on the cheek. I wrapped my Luger under my left arm, covered it with my coat and checked myself in the mirror. On my way out I told her to meet me at the Italian joint we had agreed upon at ten. She said she'd be there.

Carlene was waiting patiently at my desk when I arrived fifteen minutes late. She had on a dazzling red dress that ran down to her ankles, her hair up in an intricately braided design, and finely woven sandals.

"You're a vision," I said as greeting. "Like a being fallen from heaven."

"Mister Glacier," she grinned, "flattery won't get you anywhere with me."

"It's not flattery if it's true, my dear."

We walked hand in hand out to the street, I hailed a cab and paid with one of the fifties. The cabby wasn't impressed. He grumbled for a moment before announcing he couldn't possibly break a bill that large, and I was forced to give him a two dollar tip because he only had forty-five dollars in change.

"Bastard," I snarled, "a damn thief is what he is."

"Come on, sugar." Carlene pulled my arm gently. "Let's just go have a good time."

A large colored fellow the size of a Russian tank manned the doors, even though the club was completely dead. He sized me up, winked at Carlene and put his tree limb arm out to stop me from entering.

"I gotta frisk ya, sir," he said, his voice like gravel under tractor tires.

"Of course," I nodded, slipped a ten out of my pocket and touched his chest, softly but firm enough to drop the bill into his vest pocket. "May I ask who owns this club?"

"Mister Coronado, sir." He nodded to me, did a good job of acting like he was patting me down, but not looking for anything, and then stepped out of the way. As I moved past him, he leaned in close. "My advice is to keep that heater shelved, mister, or it'll take a lot more than ten bucks to get you outta here alive."

We took a booth in the back and ordered dinner. I found that they made a damn good steak at the Roxy, and ate it silently as I watched the club begin its business day. The place was nearly empty as Carlene and I ate. There was a bartender, a few waitresses preparing for the dinner rush, the colored man at the door, and two Negro bus-boys. No customers at all. When I finished my steak, I ordered drinks for myself and Carlene, and then excused myself to find Maxie.

"Evening," I said to the barman. "I'm looking for a girl named Maxie."

"No dames here by that name." He frowned. "Maxie's a man. He plays the piano." He gestured with his chin to a thin, bald man sitting at a grand piano on stage, adjusting his book so he could accurately read the notes. "What's this about, anyway?"

"A friend of a friend." I shrugged, and left him there to go speak with Maxie.

"Mister Maxie?"

"And you would be?" He stood and shook my hand with a weak, clammy handshake. He was small all over. Small, thin arms, small build, beady little eyes hidden under thick rimmed glasses and thin lips that were almost invisible. It struck me right away that he was queer, which left me wondering about Mr. Marx.

"My name's Rick Glacier," I said. "I'm here to talk to you about Sammy Marx."

"What about him?" His feral eyes scanned the room nervously. I looked behind me and noticed that the room was filling up. I wouldn't have much time to talk with Maxie before he had to start playing.

"He's disappeared."

"Has he?"

"He has." I nodded. "When was the last time you saw him?"

"Three days ago. Maybe four."

"His wife hasn't seen him in a week. What's your relationship with Sammy?"

"He's an admirer of my music, Mister Glacier. That's all."

"You seem a little defensive about the whole thing," I said, studied him. He was looking over my shoulder. In the reflection of his spectacles I could see two large colored men coming up behind me. A quick glance to my right and I saw a thin Italian there as well. "I'm just trying to find the man."

"And why's that?" He asked.

"His wife is worried about him." As I spoke I caught a flash to my right and ducked just in time to avoid a lead pipe as it whistled past my temple. I brought my right foot up and kicked out at my attacker, catching him in the knee and bending it backwards. My Luger was in my hand an instant later, and I spun to see the two Negros pulling revolvers. I had to make a decision.

A. Run like hell – flip to Chapter 7a.

B. Shoot the Italian, then deal with the Negros – flip to Chapter 7b.

C. Shoot the Negros first, then deal with the Italian – flip to Chapter 7c.

CHAPTER 6B

"Meet me here at seven," I told Carlene. "We'll hit the club and maybe take in a show after."

"Don't get ahead of yourself, Mister Glacier." She winked and then disappeared from the threshold.

I decided to finish what Carlene had started and mopped the rest of the floor. Then I wheeled the bucket and mop out of my office and leaned it against the door, closed up and locked it from the inside. I sat in my chair with a sigh and reflected for a bit.

It felt good to pay my rent. Finally I was getting somewhere. Maybe not far, but somewhere. When I found Sammy Marx I would be getting somewhere else entirely. Hopefully, Mrs. Marx had friends. Hopefully, she was grateful. The dame knew how to move. I figured I might be able to maneuver my way into her panties at least once more before we went our separate ways. I didn't feel real great about finding that prick though. Sammy had single handedly wiped out the city's case against Delaney, and for all I cared he could sleep with the fishes indefinitely for that. But being a PI was different from being a cop, I got paid for solving cases now, not despite them.

I leaned back in my chair and lit a smoke, closed my eyes and tried to get my mind flowing properly. The night with Melanie Marx and the day running around, talking with Carlene, paying rent and having my way with the broad from the bar had taken their toll. I slipped off into a deep, restful sleep, and didn't wake until Carlene pressed against my shoulder and shouted in my ear.

"Mister Glacier!" she growled. "We'll be late!"

I started and looked around, confused. The sun had set and the office was a pale blue in the emerging moonlight. Carlene was standing beside me in a stunning red dress, her hair braided beautifully, her feet dressed in intricately woven sandals.

"Wow," I said, "you are absolutely breathtaking."

"I know," she smirked, "now can we get going? It took me ten minutes to wake you up, and now we're late."

We walked down to the street together, hailed and a cab and took it to the Roxy. I tossed the driver six quarters for the ride and got out, Carlene's hand in mine. The place was starting to get busy and it took us a few moments to work our way to the front of the line. There was a mountain of a colored man standing guard, and as we went to pass he held up his arm and stopped me.

"I'm sorry, sir" he said in a gravelly voice, "but I'll have'ta frisk ya."

I smiled, reach into my pocket to pull out a bribe and realized I had nothing. I was flat broke. I was supposed to meet up with Mrs. Marx at seven, that was a half-hour ago, and I had spent the advance.

The mammoth spun me around and pressed me against the wall. Within seconds he found my rod and pulled it from my shoulder holster.

"I can explain that," I said.

"You got a ticket for this, mister?" he asked. I could feel his breath hot and foul against my cheek. "Cuz this is a problem."

Out of the corner of my eye, I saw three uniforms approaching. They had their hands on their hips, ready for action, and one had his Billy club out and ready.

"Is there a problem here?" the one with his flap-jack asked.

"Yeah," the Negro growled. "This man was tryin' to come into Mister Coronado's club with a rod."

"You got a ticket for that, sir?" the officer asked.

"No," I told the wall. The colored guard flipped me around to address the cops. "No, officer, I've hit on some hard times, my registration expired last month. But I'm a PI and I just got a good paying job. I'll re-register it in the morning. It's no problem."

"Rick Glacier?" the cop asked. "Well, I'll be." I recognized him then as Officer Peter Ballard, a former boxer and crooked cop who had been on Coronado's payroll since orientation.

"Come on, Ballard," I huffed. "We both know you aren't going to take me in over an expired ticket."

"No," he shook his head, and then hit me square in the stomach with his flap-jack. "I'm gonna take you in and charge your ass for trying to get into Coronado's club with a heater. Not because I think you could have done anything with it, and not because you don't have it registered, but because you're an asshole and the boss pays me real good to make sure bastards like you don't get into his club."

Pete and his pals hauled me up and put the bracelets on me. I watched as Carlene glared at me in disgust, and then spun on her magnificent sandals and walked away. I shook my head and sighed. I wouldn't be sleeping with Carlene.

I wouldn't be solving the case, which meant I wouldn't be sleeping with Melanie Marx either. And I wouldn't be paid. And I would lose my PI license. And I was out of business.

I looked around for a moment, stupidly, and then followed Ballard to his squad car, let him press my head down and push me in. Rick Glacier: PI, was over, and he hadn't lasted very long at all.

(Come on, man. This one was obvious. You were supposed to meet Mrs. Marx at seven. If you had been paying attention, you would have remembered that. This was a given. It doesn't take a rocket scientist to figure out you don't double-book a date with two equally hot chicks. Besides, this is New York, dumb-ass. You can't just walk around New York City with an unregistered Luger, even in 1950. Go back and use your head this time. Try picking a time for the date that doesn't already coincide with another date. Maybe you should start keeping a day-planner, bitch.)

CHAPTER 6C

"How about eight at my place?" I said. "I got a meeting with my client at seven. We'll meet at my apartment, have some coffee and then head out from there."

"Sounds good."

"Maybe if things go well, we'll hit a show after."

"We'll leave that up to fate, Mister Glacier." Her face disappeared from the threshold and I felt a shudder run through me. The babe did that to me. Always had.

I left the mop, bucket and puddle where she had left them and went home. I had a shower and a shave and spent an hour chain smoking and cleaning my Luger. Then I mixed myself a highball and drank it down without taking a breath. I wasn't getting anywhere and I was getting there fast.

Besides getting my rocks off, I hadn't done a damn thing worthwhile all day. Well, I got a sweet date for the night, and the address to a joint that Marx hung at, plus a name, Maxie, but that was about all. And that was a long way away from finding the elusive Mr. Marx.

That thought led me to Mrs. Marx and the fifty I would be getting each day that I kept on the hunt. This could turn into a pretty sweet gig if the guy never showed. I was just starting to hope he never would when I glanced at the clock and realized it would be a tough stretch to make it to the Italian joint on time.

The cabby was a Guinea and I didn't like his attitude. He took the long way to run up the fare and I had to think maybe that's what I was doing with the Marx case. When he dropped me at the restaurant I tossed him a hand full of dimes and listened to him gripe as I got out.

The restaurant was in the good part of town, but quaint. It really had a way of making you feeling like you were eating in some old Grandma's kitchen. The tables were dressed with checkered red cloth and the chairs were old and riddled with marks as if a dog had sharpened its teeth on them. A couple of wise guys sat around in the back corner, playing cards and smoking cigars that stunk all the way through the place.

I found Melanie at a table eating ravioli. She looked up when I walked in and motioned for the bartender to bring me a drink.

"Wine?" she asked.

I shook my head.

"You don't drink wine?"

"I'm not French," I told her, "thank God for that. I'll have bourbon with club on the rocks." The waiter disappeared and arrived back in a flash with an expertly mixed drink. I made a mental note to have Mrs. Marx hit him with a good tip. Maybe a deuce.

"So," she leaned back as I sat across from her, "what have you found?"

"Your old man likes a place called Roxy's. Ever heard of it?"

"Never." She scowled. "Sounds disreputable."

"Naw." I downed my drink and signaled for another. "I never heard of it. If it was real shady I would know. Probably a dance place, maybe a jazz club, anyway I'm going out there after I leave here. Check it out."

"Good." She placed a ravioli in her mouth, chewed a moment, then said, "Is that all?"

"Nope. I need more money. I'm tapped out."

"Already?"

"Yup. It takes money to make people talk, sister, and I ain't spending my own."

"Fine, Mister Glacier," she huffed, reached into her bag and pulled out a wad. I was starting to wonder if she had a trap door in that bag. "How's a hundred? Will that last you a few days?"

"Hundred's fine. That's not all pay though. Remember it's fifty a day plus expenses."

"That's fine. But I'll need receipts."

"Of course." Receipts? I thought about tossing ten bucks to a broad, decided not to mention it. "I'll just have to have all the snitches sign a waiver every time they give me information."

"Mister Glacier, that's not what I meant."

"Look," I sneered, "I'm just as happy as you to have what happened last night go by the way side, and I don't like waking up to sissy notes written with lipstick kisses. But that doesn't mean you treat me like a worker by day and something else by night."

"Mister Glacier," she said again, exasperated, "I don't know what you're talking about." She looked around to make sure no one heard what I had said, then leaned in and said, "What happens in private stays there."

"Whatever." I waved her off, reached across the table and took one of her butts. "Got a light?"

She tossed me a book of matches and I lit my smoke. I gave the book a glance, and tossed it back to her. Sucked the smoke deep into my lungs and finished my drink.

"I gotta go."

I took the hundred, two fifties as crisp as if they had just been pressed, and left her there without saying goodbye. Up tight, rich women and their uppity ways, they burned me up. It wasn't like I expected a kiss, but nobody treats Rick Glacier like yesterday's garbage.

The cabby was a mick and I liked him. He got me to my apartment in just a few minutes, so I tossed him a fifty and told him I only wanted forty-five in change.

"Thanks buddy," he said over his shoulder.

Melanie Marx had me in a foul mood, but it could only get better because it was eight and Carlene should be by any minute. And she was. I had barely closed the door behind me when the buzzer rang and I heard her sweet voice beckoning to come up. I pushed the button and unlocked the door. She was in my kitchen two minutes later.

"So," she sighed, "to the Roxy?"

"Not yet." I checked my watch. "I don't want to show until nine. Better that way."

"Why?"

"Because it'll be slow but about to pick up. I need everyone there but I don't want a big crowd."

She crossed the room and poured herself a drink as if she'd been in my place a hundred times. "Drink?"

"Bourbon," I told her. "Anyway you take it."

She mixed herself one with soda and pinch of lemon, then made mine the same. She looked wonderful. Good enough to eat. She had on a gown that glistened lightly in the dark gloom of my apartment. Fine shoes with tall heels that showcased her trim ankles. Her hair spilled down around her shoulders, shimmering in the light as she walked back to hand me my drink.

"Anything else?" she asked.

I dropped the glass in the sink and hauled her into my arms. She resisted for a moment, and then melted against my chest.

"That's a beautiful gown you got on," I told her. "What's under it?"

"Nothing," she breathed.

I carried her into the bedroom and gently laid her onto the sheets. Then I slowly rolled up her gown to expose her nakedness. She was breathtaking. Long, smooth legs that ran to a neatly shaved patch of curly hair in the center. I ran my hands along her thighs and felt her muscles stiffen.

"I won't hurt you, too bad," I said. She giggled. I let my tongue drag along the length of one shapely leg until I reached the dewy juncture between her quivering thighs. My tongue left a slick trail along the exposed lips, my warm breath and the feel of my tongue penetrating her delicate folds drew out a shuddering moan.

She tasted sweet as honey, and I drank her in. With the gown shoved up past her waist, I could see the muscles in her abdomen contracting with each skilled flick of my tongue. I slipped my hand beneath the bunched up material, seeking and finding the perfection of her silken breast. I kneaded it gently, keeping rhythm with my tongue, nearly sending her into convulsions when I squeezed the nipple between my finger and thumb then gave it a good, hard tug.

Her moans grew louder, her body rocking from side to side until she finally peaked, flooding my mouth with her warm nectar. When the wild thrashing subsided and her limbs went limp, I lifted my head and leveled a cocky grin at her.

"Are you ready for the Roxy?" I asked, my cheeks damp from her overflowing juices.

"My God, Rick," she gasped, "my father was right about you. You're an animal."

"A lot of people think I am." I wiped my face on the sheet. "But I'm my own brand of animal."

"To the Roxy," she said with a regretful sigh.

We took a cab and this time I didn't give a tip. I worked my way to the front of the line easily. It didn't hurt having a knockout walking next to me. A large colored man the size of Hells' Kitchen was guarding the door.

"I'll have'ta frisk ya, sir," he said. His voice was like thunder rolling across the sky.

"No problem." I slid a ten into his pocket and smiled. "Just doing your job."

He patted me down for show, ignored the obvious bulge of my Luger, and then ushered us in. Inside, the place was filling up. People were scattered here and there, talking, smoking, and starting their evening drinking. I ordered us each a bourbon and left Carlene nursing hers while I went up to the bar.

"Hey, bub," I said to the barkeep, held out a deuce. "I'm looking for a girl named Maxie."

"No girl named Maxie here," he said, and slid the two dollar bill from my fingers, "just a guy. The piano player." He pointed.

"Thanks, buddy."

"Anybody asks," he said, "I didn't talk to you."

"Of course." I left him and walked across the floor to where Maxie was trying to properly position his cords atop the piano. Maxie was a thin, bald little bastard wearing a tuxedo that looked a size too big.

"Mister Maxie?" I asked when I reached him.

"And you would be?" He stood and shook my hand with a weak, clammy handshake. He was small all over. Small, thin arms, small build, beady little eyes hidden under thick rimmed glasses and thin lips that were almost invisible. It struck me right away that he was queer, which left me wondering about Mr. Marx.

"My name's Rick Glacier," I said. "I'm here to talk to you about Sammy Marx."

"What about him?" His rat-like eyes scanned the room nervously. I looked behind me and noticed that the room was almost full. I wouldn't have much time to talk with Maxie before he had to start playing.

"He's disappeared."

"Has he?"

"He has," I nodded, "when was the last time you saw him?"

"Three days ago. Maybe four."

"His wife hasn't seen him in a week. What's your relationship with Sammy?"

"He's an admirer of my music, Mister Glacier. That's all."

"You seem a little defensive about the whole thing," I said, studied him. He was looking over my shoulder. In the reflection of his spectacles I could see two large colored men coming up behind me. A quick glance to my right and I saw a thin Italian there as well. "I'm just trying to find the man."

"And why's that?" he asked.

"His wife is worried about him." As I spoke I caught a flash to my right and ducked just in time to avoid a lead pipe as it whistled past my temple. I brought my right foot up and kicked out at my attacker, catching him in the knee and bending it backwards. My Luger was in my hand an instant later, and I spun to see the two Negros pulling revolvers. I had to make a decision.

A. Run like hell – flip to Chapter 7a.

B. Shoot the Italian, then deal with the Negros – flip to Chapter 7b.

C. Shoot the Negros, then deal with the Italian – flip to Chapter 7c.

CHAPTER 7A

I took one look at the guys coming at me, the guns in their hands, the look in their eyes and I ran like hell. I could hear Carlene screaming something I couldn't understand as I burst through the door to the left of stage and took off down the hall.

Behind the stage was a labyrinth system of corridors that led from one back room to another. I hit each door but none opened. I didn't try the knobs, just hit them with my shoulder and hoped they'd give. None did, so I kept moving. I could hear the footsteps of my pursuers behind me, pounding on the cement floor as they ran.

At the end of one hall I saw a door with a sign lit up bright red. "EXIT" it said, and I made for it. I ran and turned and slammed my shoulder into it and it gave and I tumbled out onto the pavement. I was in the alley behind the club, so I turned right and ran with all my might to get to the street. If I could catch a cab, I was home free.

As I rounded the corner I heard a click and a bang and felt something hit me in the back. It hit me so hard I doubled over and rolled three feet before coming to a halt. The Italian came limping into view, following the colored doorman sporting a sawed-off shotgun and a nasty grin. He looked down into my eyes, as everything started to go white.

"So that's Rick Glacier," he said.

"*Was*," the Italian nodded. "Not no more."

(Are you flippin' kidding me? "Run like hell." That's your answer? This is Rick Glacier! He's not going to run from an [American of Italian Decent] and a couple of [African American]'s! He's big and he's cold! He's a man! If we had lilies like you fighting for us in the War we'd all be speaking Jap and Jerry right now. Go back and man up. I don't care who you shoot, but shoot somebody. Fucking pussy.)

CHAPTER 7B

I turned on my heel and shot the Italian straight in the mug. The bullet opened up the top of his head and sprayed his brains, pasty gray, all over the stage. I heard screaming from around me and saw the club was quickly becoming a mob scene. Everyone was making for the door at once. All but the colored boys coming at me, guns raised but hindered by the pressing crowd.

I sighted down my trusty Luger and put a bullet right through the eye of one of them. I watched as the lead bored through and sprang from the back of his head, covering a finely dressed woman with blood and bone and brains. The guy behind him wasn't impressed. He pushed the woman out of the way as she cried and sobbed, pawing at her face to get the sticky stuff from her cheeks. Dropped to a knee, sighting down his chubby revolver at me.

I didn't give him a stagnant target. I sprang up and wrapped an arm around Maxie, who'd gone white as powdered sugar. I used him as a shield and for some reason the Negro didn't fire. We crossed together to the side door that led off the stage, and then I pushed him in front of me and we ran to the door with the "EXIT" sign at the end of the corridor. Maxie wasn't much of a sprinter, but the gun in his back encouraged him move pretty quick.

We burst into the night and Maxie crumpled onto the pavement. I hauled him up and we were moving again. We made it to the end of the alley and I turned left and saw the fellow I had paid off coming at me with a scatter gun. I really didn't want to shoot him, he seemed like a nice enough guy, but I buried three rounds in his chest anyway. He stumbled a few feet and then fell flat on his face. He hadn't done anything but pick the wrong employer, but I would rather see him get dead than get clipped myself.

I looked right and saw a couple getting out of a car. The dame was sitting in the passenger seat, waiting for her old man to open the door. I shoved him out of the way and deposited Maxie in the back seat. The broad was screaming and the thought of kicking her out crossed my mind, but I was short on time so I apologized and swept into the driver's seat beside her.

"I'm a cop, lady, don't worry," I said, and spun the wheel to get off the curb. The guy was yelling and practically frothing at the mouth, but I left him behind and crossed in front of the club. "I'm looking for my date," I explained to the frightened hostage, "she's... there she is!"

"Carlene!" I shouted out the window. "Here! Carlene!" She saw me flagging her and ran to the car. "Maxie, open the damned door!"

He did, and she poured in. I jammed the accelerator to the floor turned right and then left and then right again, trying to put as much illogical distance between us and the club as possible. The girl beside me was shaking but calming down.

"Who's she?" Carlene asked.

"She came with the car. Don't worry, doll," I told my reluctant passenger. "I'll let you out soon. We just have to find a safe place and then we'll catch a cab and you'll be on your merry way."

"What's going on?" Her voice said she was slightly afraid, slightly aroused, and mostly curious.

"The dame's a friend," I explained, "my date to the Roxy. This feller's the piano player from the Roxy, and I'm the guy who just shot three men back there."

"Really?"

"Really. But I didn't want to do it. They were trying to kill me. Better them than me. That's the first rule of being a private investigator: sometimes people need to die. But it should never be me."

"That makes sense."

"Makes sense to me, babe, and that's all that counts."

"So," Carlene asked from the back, "where are we going?"

"I don't know yet. They knew who they were after, so they'll hit my place soon enough. I doubt they know where you live, but your pops wouldn't like it too much if we went there."

"Nope."

"We can go to my place," the girl said. "My husband'll be filing paperwork all night. He loves this car, he won't be very happy about you stealing it."

"What about you?" I asked. "He won't be worried about you?"

"Less than the car. Trust me." She laughed bitterly. "He'll just assume he can get another one of me."

"Well I'll be damned." I couldn't believe a thing like that. "What do you broads see in guys like that?"

"Money," the girls said as one.

"I'll be damned," I said again. "Okay, we'll go to your place. What's your name, anyway?"

"Grace."

"Okay Grace, we're going to your place." I repeated, collecting my thoughts. "Point me in the right direction."

She pointed and followed it up with words. She was a damn good navigator, turns out. She got us there in minutes and we left the car parked and locked outside of a brownstone that looked to be new.

She led us inside, Maxie still had a gun in his back, and into a foyer with slabs of granite for floors and marble pillars. The furniture was gold painted and well padded. There was a small bar to one side that looked custom made for entertaining people while they waited to see the master of the house, and I fixed myself a drink and one for each of the ladies.

"I'll take a scotch," Maxie said.

"No, you won't," I told him. "You'll answer my questions and if you don't I'll smear your blood all over this nice floor here, and Grace can tell the cops somebody stole her man's car, took her to this house, and killed a man right in front of her. It'll get her lots of sympathy at all the social outings."

"I won't tell them who," she added. "I like Rick. He's the kind of man I wish my husband could be."

"See there," I pointed at her, "that's a nice thing to say. You got any nice things to say, Maxie?"

"What'd'ya want to know?" he blustered.

"First, why were those boys trying so hard to kill me?"

"I don't know. That's Mister Coronado's business. I don't get involved."

"But you know Sammy."

"Yes... yes I do."

"How well?"

"What?"

"How well do you know him?" I leaned against the wall, sipped my drink, the pistol still pointed at his gut. "I mean, I would say I don't know you real well. I know Carlene here okay, and Grace barely at all. So would you say you know him well, okay, in passing, or not at all?"

"Pretty well."

"Are you queer for each other?"

"What?"

"Stop saying 'what.' It gets on my nerves. I'm the one who asks questions. When you ask me 'what?' it makes me feel like you're interrogating me and I don't like that. So, answer the question, are you two queer for each other."

"I assure you..."

"Okay, so you are. It's not a big deal. We're all friends here. I'm sure Missus Marx'll take it pretty hard, but hey, not my problem."

"But... no one can know. It would ruin us both."

"I don't think anyone has doubts about you, friend. You're more fag than a pack of English cigarettes."

I pushed myself off the wall and made another drink. The alcohol was taking the edge off my nerves that killing three men had put on them. I've never liked killing before, but I've never had a real problem with it either. I drank down half my bourbon and then leaned back against the wall. The ladies were huddled together, enjoying the show.

"So, when's the last time you saw Sammy?"

"Three days ago, maybe four."

"You already told me that. I didn't believe you then, and I don't believe you now." I wiggled the Luger. "When?"

"This morning," he shook his head, "I saw him this morning."

"This morning?" I asked. The girls' eyes lit up. "You saw him this morning? When?"

"Breakfast. He came by to have breakfast with me."

"So, where's he now?"

"I don't know. He wouldn't tell me." A shudder ran through him and his head wouldn't stop shaking from side to side. I got the impression he was ready for a complete meltdown. "He's scared as anything. He's hiding out someplace and only comes by with an armed guard."

"Really?" I made my way over to the bar and poured him a scotch. "Who's got the guard on him?"

"Mister Coronado," he said, took the drink from my hand and downed it.

"Really?" I asked again. "So Coronado's got something on him, then."

"Yeah," he nodded somberly, "me."

"Gotcha. But that means Coronado swiped him and he's holding him for Delaney's books."

"No," he shook his head again. I started to wonder how it stayed on with all that shaking. "Coronado didn't swipe him, Sammy asked for protection."

"From Delaney?"

"Yup. Roger put a hit out on him. Don't know why, but Sammy came to the club all upset a few nights ago..."

"A week?"

"Yeah, a week ago, and asked to see Mister Coronado. He didn't tell me what was happening 'til the next day at lunch. He's scared as anything," he said again.

"Fine," I nodded, "that'll do."

"That's all I know, Mister, I swear it."

"I believe you, Maxie. I do." I crossed the room and pulled him out of the chair. We walked together to the door and I tossed him out. "Now I suggest you don't go back to that club. Coronado'll know you talked just by lookin at ya. And he'll have questions of his own. Hide out and when this thing's over, find a place that isn't mobbed up to make a living."

I slammed the door in his face and turned to the dames. They were all keyed up to see what came next. I let out a stream of four letter words that wasn't right to say in front of women and made myself another drink. Mrs. Marx was going to get a visit, and it wouldn't be as pleasant as our last.

"So…" Carlene began. "What now?"

"I'm taking you home." I downed the bourbon with a grimace and looked at her. "Grace, you can say whatever you want. Just don't mention me or the babe. That's all I ask."

"I'll say a couple of blacks took the car and I fought them off." She shrugged. "Who knows. Maybe I'll just tell them my husband's drunk and running off at the mouth."

I laughed. "That'll really make his day."

"Anyway, he won't be home for a bit, like I said, so if you two want to stay for a while," she shrugged again, "that's okay with me."

I got the impression she meant more than just having an easy drink with nice company, and I crossed the room and took her into my arms. She resisted for a split second, enough to say that she didn't like the idea of infidelity, and then she went slack and looked up at me with big, doe eyes.

"Mister Glacier," she said softly, "I'm a good, Christian woman."

"I know, kid, but sometimes Christian women need men who are interested in more than money and cars." I kissed her then, full on the mouth, and she kissed me back. Carlene came over and kissed her next. They kissed tenderly, and it was like Hiroshima in my head. I rubbed their backs as their tongues playfully teased each other's senses.

Carlene lost her clothes first. The gown dropped to the granite floor in a neat, ruffled heap and I smiled at her nakedness. She was maddeningly beautiful. Her breasts were small but full and Grace bent down and suckled them like a hungry baby. I ran my hand through her hair as she did, feeling myself grow stiff.

Grace sucked and licked and teased the nipple. Carlene rocked her head back and kissed me, hard. There was so much passion in her eyes I thought I might get burned. I kissed her back, letting my hand glide over her neglected breast and down to her flat belly.

"Grace," my voice was almost a whisper, "lose the dress."

She did. She slipped the straps off her shoulders and did an erotic little shimmy that sent the dress slithering down over her hips to pool at her feet, allowing me to drink in her beauty. I did, and suddenly felt more of a drunkard than I ever had with whiskey. Beneath her gown was a black brassiere and matching black panties, hooked to stockings with a small black band. The cloth separated between her legs, leaving her sex exposed. Two small, white lips ran below a heart-shaped patch of red hair.

I led them through the foyer to a sitting room, kissing playfully as we went. Carlene stretched out on the plush sofa, purring like a kitten when Grace eagerly dipped her head between Carlene's thighs and began licking her. I unsnapped the brassiere let her breasts hang free, and what magnificent breasts they were. The size of a small melon, they were full and round with small, erect nipples that begged to be bitten. I ran my hand along her back, down the crevice that led to her ass, and entered her with my fingers.

She barely flinched as I pressed three big, meaty fingers into her and began stroking her from behind. Carlene moaned as Grace brought her to a climax while I continued to stroke Grace until she was hot and wet, then slowly impaled her with my throbbing phallus.

She was tighter than a Jew's billfold but she opened easier and took me inside her like a seasoned whore, pushing back each time I surged forward, her ass slapping against my thighs as I pumped harder and faster. Her moans of pleasure were almost as arousing as the inner muscles that clamped around my member as if they'd never let go, and it didn't take long before the grand finale exploded. Her body quivered uncontrollably as I let out a primal grunt and drained myself inside her, and even after I'd pulled out and sat down, Grace continued to moan. She'd stopped licking on Carlene, though her head was on Carlene's lap, and her delightful rear was still wiggling in the air like a hotel sign with a vacancy to be filled.

I lit a smoke. "Carlene," I said, "when I get my breath back, you're next."

"Yes, sir," she breathed. "Anything my man asks."

(Continue to Chapter 8)

CHAPTER 7C

I ignored the Italian writhing around on the stage, grasping his busted knee, and tracked my pistol through the crowd. When I had the two colored boys in my sights, I opened up my Luger and let them have every last round in the clip. I aimed low, and took out their legs in one long hail of gunfire. I watched them drop one after the other as the lead bored through them, cutting cartilage and sinew, shattering bone. I pulled that little metal trigger until the firing pin struck dumb and the slide lay open above the grip. One of the blacks got hit in the neck as he went down, his throat opening up and spraying a thick stream of bright red across the crowd.

They fired as they dropped, and to my right I heard a grunt as Maxie took a slug to the left corner pocket. His blood sprayed across my face as his skull opened with the force of the explosion, but I didn't stop to wipe it off. I grabbed up the Italian and used his body as a shield. With my free arm I slapped another clip in my Luger and tracked the second black as he tried to hobble up on one of his ruined legs. I shot him twice in the chest, watched him drop like a sack of potatoes and then took off for the stage door, hauling the Italian behind me.

The guy was thin and didn't weight much, but he made up for it by dragging that bum leg behind him like an anchor. I had to press the gun into his back so hard he whinnied like an unhappy pony, and I smacked him in the back of the head with it so he'd get the right idea.

We smashed through the door with the "EXIT" sign at the end of the corridor and poured out into the alley that ran behind the club. The gangster dropped on his wounded knee, and once again I had to haul him up and force him to follow. He cursed and spat as I pulled him along, his leg outstretched as straight as he could keep it, hobbling on the other while his hands clutched his bad knee.

"Where are you taking me?" he asked through forced breaths.

"Quiet," I snarled, and raked him across the face with my Luger.

Up ahead, the alley opened to the street and I stopped to get my bearings. To my left was the mountainous doorman I had given ten good bucks for nothing. He had a pump-action shotgun in his hands. He shouted something I couldn't hear through rush of adrenaline and then fell as a horizontal hail of hot lead filled him and split open his guts, pouring them onto the sidewalk in a burst of blood and steam. Smoke curled from my Luger like the end of a smoldering cigarette.

I spun on my heal and caught sight of a colored girl standing by the curb, smoking and standing like she was waiting for someone. I ran to her, my hostage in tow, and told her we needed a ride.

"I ain't got no car, Mister." She blew smoke in my face. "Call a damn cab."

I stuffed a ten in her cleavage.

"Look, babe, we need a ride right now," I said. "There's ten more in it for you. Please."

She smiled, checked the cash, and then nodded. It didn't take her but a moment to flag down an elderly man in a cashmere sweater driving a Cadillac the size of a battle-cruiser. I stayed in the shadows of a doorway and waited. I could hear the commotion outside the club as new men were recruited to find me, my hostage, and finish the job the others had failed to do.

I watched the Negro girl wiggle her ass, and figured it was as good a time as any. I gave the Italian a good slug to the face and dragged him, nearly unconscious, across the walk and threw him in the back seat of the Cadillac. The driver was too stunned to object. That is until I ripped him out of the driver's seat and got in after him.

"Get in," I told the street walker.

"I ain't coming with you."

"You want your ten?"

She grumbled something and got in. I slammed down on the accelerator and pulled away from the curb. I put a block between us and the club, and then turned around.

"Watcha doin?" the dame asked. "I thought we were tryin' to get away from this place."

"I gotta find my date." I leaned in close to the steering column, trying to obscure my features with the wheel. We passed the old guy, standing in the street, waving his hands grandiosely in the air, explaining what had happened to one of Coronado's thugs.

"There!" I pointed. "Carlene! Carlene, here!"

She was in the back seat next to the Guinea and we were moving before anyone on the street knew what was happening. I made a series of left and right turns with no logical reasoning in an attempt to arrive in the most out of the way place I could as quickly as possible.

"Well," Carlene said from behind me, "that was interesting."

"Very." I nodded. "You're in some deep mud, bub." I looked at the gangster through the rear-view mirror. "What's your name, anyway?"

"Tony."

"Of course it is." I nodded.

"While we're introducing ourselves, who the heck are you?" The colored girl asked.

"I'm Rick Glacier, private investigator."

"A damned dick." She shook her head, turned to the back seat. "And what kind of a name is Carlene?"

"It's my name," Carlene spat. "What's your name?"

"Rose."

"Oh," Carlene shrugged, "I guess there's nothing wrong with that."

"Ladies." I raised my hands, thought better of it and put them back on the wheel. "Let's not start taking out the claws. We're all on the same side here. Except for Tony."

"Where'd you get her?" Carlene asked. I could hear the slightest edge of jealousy in her voice.

"She helped us find a ride, that's all."

"And I expect to be paid."

"Yeah, yeah. Don't worry so much. First we have to find a place to dump the car and ask Tony some questions."

"Don't look at me," Rose laughed. "My neighborhood'll be the first place they look for a stolen car."

"True." I nodded. "And we can't go back to my place..."

"My old man's home," Carlene added.

"My leg is seriously hurt," Tony complained. "I think I need to see a doctor."

"A hotel." I ignored him. "But no matter where we go we'll attract attention. Three white folks and a black girl in this giant crate," I shook my head, "the cops are the least of our problems."

"My brother could take the car," Rose offered. "Of course, it'd cost you a few more dollars, but he'd get rid of it for you."

"You mean he'll chop it up and make a bundle off of it."

"Not my business, man." She looked out the window. "Twenty more bucks, I'll get rid of the car."

"Fine." I counted off thirty and handed it to her. "Drop us off at the hotel, and go get rid of the car."

"Whoa," she put her hands up defensively. "No, that's not how it works. I'm not running off in this car so you can call the boys in blue and let me take the fall for it. We stay together, that's that."

"Fine," I let out a string of curses and tried to assemble a plan. "We'll drop you at the hotel. You get a room. Carlene, go with her. Once you have a room number and two sets of keys, Carlene will come back out and the three of us will go in together. Rose, you'll meet us in the room. Sound good?"

They said it did, and everyone followed instructions and for the first time in my life everything went as planned. The clerk looked at Tony's leg and at me, and I smiled and said he fell playing a pick-up game of stickball and we were just going to get him fixed up before sending him home to his wife.

"Don't let 'im bleed on my sheets," she said through a fog of tobacco smoke. "Or I'll charge ya an extra fifty cents for the cleaning."

I stuck Tony in a wobbly little chair in the corner, the only piece of furniture in the room other than the bed and a little end table. Rose sat down on the bed, Carlene beside her. They had been far friendlier since they accompanied each other alone at check-in.

"Babes," I said, "you might want to go for a walk. This might get ugly."

"We'll watch." Rose smiled. "I don't wanna miss any action."

"Yeah," Carlene nodded, "and this guy tried to take your head off with that pipe, remember? I don't like him much after that."

"There you have it, Tony," I said, "I have to agree with her."

"What the hell you want from me?" he asked. "I'm just an errand boy, I don't know nuthin."

"Everybody knows something," I told him, "and since Maxie is no longer in the land of the living, I'm going to ask you the questions I was going to ask him." I leaned against the wall and took a flask out of my pocket. "There's two ways this can go down. One: you can tell me what you know, answer every question I ask, and I'll let you go. Two: I'm gonna beat you real bad, I might even cut ya a little bit. Then when I'm done, I'm gonna drop you right on Coronado's door-step. You know why?"

"Why?"

"So that he can ask you questions next. And he will. He'll ask what questions I asked, and when you're afraid to tell him how much you told me, he'll beat you worse than I did. And when he's finally done, he'll kill you and make sure nobody finds you."

"People saw me come in with you. If I disappear, the cops will come looking for you."

"Oh," I shook my head, "places like this don't usually do a lot of talking to the Johnny cops, Tony. That's why we're here. Besides, they wouldn't come here looking for you."

"But you took me from the club."

"Says who?" I lit a smoke and handed my flask to the girls. They were staring in wide eyed anticipation of the first blow. "But that can be fixed, too. I'll drop you at a hospital. How's that? Drop you there, and say you were in an accident, or that you tried to kill me at the Roxy, which you did. Then after the doc's are done with you, I'll be home free, and Coronado'll make you disappear."

He called me names that the ladies shouldn't have had to hear, and I smacked him in the mouth. Carlene gave me back my flask, and I put it in my pocket. I used the motion to pull my Luger.

"Now," I brought the barrel of my piece across his cheek and repeated myself. "Now, I'm going to ask you some questions. Can we begin?"

He cursed again and I hit him again. As I was wiping my hand on his shirt to clean the blood, Rose handed me something over my shoulder. It was a six inch long, well made, razor sharp, switch-blade.

"Very nice, Rose," I admired. "Are you offering this to me?"

"Just to borrow." She smiled.

"That's my girl."

I touched it to Tony's good knee. He flinched.

"Come on Tony," I said. "Or I'll run it along this tendon, that'll make you crippled for life. You don't want to be a gimp, do you?"

"What the hell do you want to know?" he whined. "Just ask the damn questions, already!"

"Let's start with the easy stuff. Why'd you try to kill me?"

"Why'd'ya think? Boss told me and the boys to take you out."

"Right there in the club? Seems risky."

"I don't know."

"Why? Why did he want me taken out?"

"I don't know," he said again. "I just follow orders, man, that's all."

"Sammy Marx come in to the Roxy a lot?"

"Yeah, I guess so...."

"Some of Delaney's girls seemed to think Sam was going there to see a girl named Maxie."

"Yeah," he laughed, "they'd think that."

"What?"

"Maxie and Sam, yeah, they're together."

"What?" I asked again.

"They make it like they're just real good friends, like Sammy is a fan of the guy's music, but we all know. I caught 'em practically eating each other's tongues once," he shuddered, "really messed me up. When I told Mister Coronado he said 'don't worry bout it' and that was it. I've never said a thing since."

"So that's what Coronado's got on Sammy." I nodded. "Maxie said he hadn't seen Sam in three or four days, but couldn't remember exactly. Missus Marx said she hadn't seen him in a week. Seems like an easy question, but why would Maxie get it wrong?"

"Because it's a lie." Tony looked at me, and shrugged. "He saw him yesterday. Maybe even today, but I know they saw each other for breakfast yesterday." He thought for a second. "In fact, probably this morning, too. I seem to remember Sam making a big thing about not missing breakfast with Max. They probably do it every morning."

"And you know this because...?"

"I took him. I was his bodyguard. But don't bother askin' me where the boss is keeping him, because I don't know. The man was already at the club when the boss asked me to bring him over to Maxie's."

"Okay," I nodded, "I believe you. But why? Why is Sammy with Coronado? He planning a hit on Delaney and needs Sam so he can control the books?"

"That's the only thing that makes sense. Like I said, I don't know. But I think Sammy went to him. I remember him coming in a week ago, he was all shaky and asked to see the boss. After that, he was in our custody. I'm guessing Delaney put a hit out on him, and he came to us for protection."

"Smart."

"Yeah."

"Okay, Tony." I helped him up. "That'll do. Now, I suggest you rethink your current career. When Coronado finds you, and he most likely will, he's not going to be real happy with you."

"I know."

"So, here's what I'm offering." I handed him my flask, and explained while he drank. "Wait here with us, we'll go and dump the car, and then I'll shoot you in the shoulder..."

"What?" He nearly coated me with bourbon. "No way, man."

"Fine." I took back my flask. "Good luck."

I pushed him out of the room and locked the door behind him. Then I turned to the ladies, who still sat on the bed. They had a different look in their eyes now. A look that said they were very comfortable being together on the bed.

"Well, babes," I said. "I guess it's time to get outta here."

Rose looked at the clock. She said, "We still have an hour or so paid for."

"Do we?" I asked. For the first time I noticed how stunning her deep brown skin was. It was so smooth that it looked like she bathed in milk four times a day. Like smooth, beaten chocolate. Suddenly I wanted to taste her. I had never had a black woman before, and I always liked trying new things. "How should we spend it?"

Even though somewhere in the deep recesses of my mind I saw it coming. Even as in my deepest, most incredible fantasies this had happened over and over. Even though it took them long agonizing moments to grow closer and closer. When the dame's lips touched and their tongues flicked out, dancing playfully with each other, it still felt like Pearl Harbor in my pants, so many simultaneous explosions the roar of them drowned out the sound of my heart pummeling the inside of my chest.

My clothes suddenly felt stifling, the temperature rising twenty degrees as I watched Carlene's elegant hands gently cup Rose's breasts, her thumbs playing across the peaks until they pebbled and strained against the fabric of Rose's blouse. I moved a little closer, a silent observer to the foreplay of teasing tongues and tentative exploration.

Carlene slid her palms up beneath Rose's shirt, stroking her bosom where I couldn't see. Then both hands rose to the colored girl's shoulders, and then higher, and Rose's shirt rose with them, up over her head, and then was dropped to the stained carpet.

It was marvelous. Rose had two large, perfectly symmetrical breasts, each about the size of a grapefruit. I couldn't imagine how she had hidden them inside the brassiere, or why she would have wanted to. Carlene snapped off the brassiere, and dropped that on the floor next. I couldn't stand idle any longer.

I stooped next to Carlene and we each took one of those beautiful breasts into our mouths. Rose tasted like sex should taste. She was warm and inviting and tasted like stale cigarettes, sweat and woman. I wrapped my mouth around her nipple and sucked and licked and bit and teased it. I heard her laugh and Carlene leaned forward and kissed her again.

"Carlene," I breathed, "lose the dress."

She did, and as she did Rose took off her skirt and they lay on the bed and played and flirted. I slid them so that I had access to both, and then let my pants fall loose and entered Rose as she and Carlene kissed.

She was easy to penetrate but hadn't been too badly abused, her inner muscles still tight enough to milk out incredible pleasure as I drove myself into her ebony body. I gave her several good, hard strokes, maintaining the pace until I felt her muscles begin to contract, then pulled out just before she went nuts. I turned to Carlene and flipped her over, gripped her hips and hoisted them up so I could enter her from behind. She was tighter than a politician's necktie but loosened almost as easily and her wild moans made me grow even harder as she squirmed and gyrated her hips in an attempt to take the full length of me inside.

Rose let out a frustrated sigh and glared at me through those cold, brown eyes. She fondled herself to keep busy while she watched me pound into Carlene. I loved the way Carlene's soft ass felt as it smacked against my thighs, loved the feel of her womb cushioning the head of my penis as I plunged deeper and deeper. But I wasn't ready for it to end. When I'd driven her almost to the point of no return, I jerked myself out and pushed Rose onto her back, pinning her arms above her head while I impaled her with one powerful thrust after another.

"Rick," Carlene cried, "stop teasing us!"

Satisfying two women at the same time wasn't difficult, it just took a little more effort and a bit of in and out synchronization. While I stuck it to Rose, I fingered Carlene, diving into both women then retreating and diving back in again. It didn't take five minutes to have Rose writhing beneath me, screaming as she came then rolling listlessly onto her side to watch as I finished Carlene off. Afterwards, they showed their appreciation, taking turns with their talented mouths and tongues, kissing, sucking, riding me until I felt the walls crashing down and let them know the curtain was closing.

I stood in front of them and used Carlene's hand to finish. As I lost control, the girl took over and I looked down lovingly as both ladies took an equal share of my seed, and then licked it off of each other's face. They rolled it into balls on their tongues and then kissed and swapped it back and forth. I sat down in the chair Tony had sat in just an hour before, and smoked and watched them finish their game, and then sadly, were forced to dress.

"Well, babes," I said again. "That was some evening."

"Yes, it was, Mister Glacier." Rose smiled and gave me a peck on the cheek. "For a dick, you sure know how to please a lady."

(Continue to Chapter 8)

CHAPTER 8

I gave Carlene a kiss that lasted a little too long to be proper, and then told the cabby to take me back to my place. He didn't know where that was, so I gave him the address. It was late and I was tired. I couldn't think much more. I needed a few good hours sleep, and some coffee and eggs in the morning, and then hopefully everything would start to make sense.

The problem was I needed to talk with Melanie Marx. I didn't really have a choice, and if she was at my place I couldn't just put it off until the next day. I would have to talk to her. She would want to know her money was being well spent, and that meant I needed to come up with excuses for what I had been doing the past few hours. It was also bound to come up that her husband was alive, was queer, and wasn't really missing in that he didn't want to be found.

That basically meant the case was closed and I owed her some money. I had it, that wasn't the problem. I just didn't want to give her tomorrow's money back. I needed to keep it. So I needed the case not to be closed. All of that meant I needed Sammy Marx to be straight, in grave danger, and desperately waiting for the moment he was reunited with his beloved wife, who would then pay me a hefty reward.

That sounded real good. But it also sounded dishonest and prone to failure. Because unless I planned on making sure Sammy never made it home, it was eventually going to be found out that Sammy was a fag and staying hid to save his own tail and keep laying it to a man's. And it would eventually lead back to me knowing he was queer and not caring. And then I would look like a sleazy PI who took his client's money and blew it on broads and booze and smokes. And even if that was technically true, it didn't make a great advertising pitch.

But that was only if I gave a damn about Mrs. Marx's feelings. I wasn't entirely sure I did. Which was the other thing I really didn't want to think or talk about. Melanie Marx had come to me and asked me to find her husband. She had been worried sick about him. She had done *anything* it took to get me on the case. She had called Sammy charming, then jealous, but anything but abnormal. Now he was a certified sexual deviant. She had said Delaney would never put a hit out on the guy. Now I knew he not only *would*, but *did*. Add to that the fact she was screwing Roger Delaney, and it was looking less and less like she wanted her husband back, and more and more like she was looking to find him so she could end her marriage the biblical way.

"That'll be five bucks, feller," the cabby said. I looked at his reflection in the rear-view.

"Five?"

"Yup, you're payin for the lady too, right?"

"Yeah," I grumbled, "I'm paying for the dame." I tossed him a crumpled up five spot and got out of the car. I didn't feel jolly enough to give any kind of tip. My Luger felt heavy under my arm. My brain felt cold and my thoughts were thick and didn't want to flow directly from one port to another. It took me two tries to get my key in and turned the proper direction, and when I stumbled into my kitchen I was greeted with the silhouette of a woman sitting at my kitchen table smoking cigarettes out of a holder.

I sighed. It didn't look like I was getting much chance to figure things out. I had to make a decision, now.

A. Tell her about the gun-fight, leave out her husband's a femme, maybe even get laid, deal with the rest in the morning – flip to Chapter 9a.

B. Tell her everything, then take out the Luger and have her answer some questions as well – flip to Chapter 9b.

C. Tell her nothing at all, walk right past her and go to bed, everything will wait until morning – flip to Chapter 9c.

CHAPTER 9A

"Look, babe," I said, "it's late, I got shot at tonight, killed three men, and I don't feel like doing much talking. So, how's about we hit the sheets and work off a little aggression?"

"You were shot at?" she gasped. I couldn't see the look on her face but I could imagine it as a mixture of terror and arousal. What she said next confirmed it. "And you killed three men?"

"Yup." I nodded, not sure if she could see it in the dark. "Which means I'm sore and tired."

"But..." she let her question hang in the air like the smoke that swirled around her shadowy face, "did you find anything out?"

"I found out someone wants me dead." I lit a smoke and leaned against the jamb. I didn't want to have this conversation. Not now, not when I couldn't see her face. Not when I felt like I was the one being questioned, because I was. "So, yup, found something out."

"But... why would anyone want you dead? I don't understand!"

"There's lots of reasons to want a man dead. With this one I would say it's because someone doesn't want your husband found."

"Does that mean he's alive?"

"It means what it means, babe, and I'll find out exactly what that is. But right now, I just need to hit the sheets, get some rest, work off some aggression. Would that be alright?"

"That's fine, Mister Glacier." She stood from the chair and crossed to me, leaned in close so that I could taste the sweetness of the tobacco she had been smoking. "How about I make you feel all better?"

"A massage'd be nice," I grumbled, "that's for sure. And probably the least you could do after the day I had on your account."

"You just come right in with me to the bedroom," she cooed. "Let's take these dirty clothes off you."

"Might want a shower." It was all I could do to mumble into my chest by that point, I was lucky I wasn't drooling like one of those "social security" types. I kept it together enough to snap my head up and say, "Yeah, a shower would be good."

"A nice hot shower is perfect," she nodded, "soften up those muscles."

She helped me into the shower and turned it on, hot enough to melt lead. I soaked under it for what felt like six hours but was probably more like fifteen minutes, maybe five. What did it matter? By the time I got out I was feeling better and even a little awake. My skin was steaming as I stepped out into the bedroom, the lights too dim to see anything more than the shifting shadows of Melanie Marx preparing herself and the room for something "special."

"Have a seat on the bed, Rick." I could hear the smile in her voice. "You won't need your towel."

The sound of her voice told me that there was no need, and better yet, a good damned reason not to be wearing it. The towel suddenly felt oppressively coarse against my skin. I dropped it to the floor and slid onto the bed.

In the darkness she was just a shadow, but her fluid movements were obviously that of a beautiful woman who had a plan. I watched the silhouette float over me, and felt my thick wrists pulled above my head by soft, dainty hands. Then I felt something cold and heard the cold metallic "click" of handcuffs being closed and tightened.

"What the...?"

"It's all part of the game." Again, her voice smiled at me from the shadows.

"What game?" I stammered. "I thought this was supposed to be a massage."

"There's something you're not telling me, Mister Glacier." Her voice was getting colder, more authoritative, more menacing with every moment that I couldn't see her facial expression. She was like a ghost, a phantom in the darkness, and I was now that specter's prisoner. "I don't like to be lied to."

"Listen, kid, I don't answer questions, I ask 'em. Now take these cuffs off or I'll tan that pretty hide of yours."

"Oh," she laughed sarcastically, "I don't think that will be happening. Those are *your* handcuffs, Mister Private Investigator, and I would assume they're left over from your days on the beat. Are they strong?" I felt her give them a little tug, proving her point. "Stronger than you?"

"Nothing's stronger than me, babe. I'm as big as they come."

Something touched my manhood and I flinched. Then I heard her take in a deep breath and let out a long, wicked chuckle.

"Yes," she said softly, "yes I think you are."

I bit back a groan when her fingers curled around me, her soft hand moving up and down my shaft in long, languishing strokes for several agonizing minutes. It was even more agonizing when the temptress took her hand away. I tried to sit up and make her keep going, but I was hindered by the restraints.

"Don't get too excited," she said coolly. "We have plenty of time."

"This is torture, you know that? It's so against the law that..."

"Oh, I'm certain you won't mind it."

"...I'll see to it you never see the light of day," I continued, ignored her taunt. "I'll shove you so deep into the system that you'll be getting screwed by bull-dikes the rest of your life!"

"Is that what your victims say to you?"

I cursed at her but she just laughed. The names I called her weren't proper in even the black districts. The viler my insults got, the more amused she became, her laughter as sexy as it was sinister. Only after I stopped struggling and fell back against the mattress, too exhausted to continue my tirade, did those petal soft fingers begin working their magic again.

"Now," she said at last, "what did you find out?"

"Nothing."

"Something. You went to the Roxy, didn't you?"

"Yup," my breath caught as she rubbed my tip, "and they shot at me. I wasn't there but a few minutes and I had three guys after me."

"Why?" She stopped stroking me again, and ran her hand down my leg, gently massaging the rippled muscles. "Was it something you said?"

"Yeah, I'd assume so. I said 'I'm looking for Sammy Marx' and that was it. They came after me just about then."

"Tell me about the Roxy." She dug her fingers into my thigh and I winced. She was a real devil, one moment her hands felt like angels caressing me, the next they felt like demons burring inside me. I would have to keep her in mind the next time I needed someone interrogated.

"It's a club, like I said. It's owned by Vito Coronado, Delaney's competition. For some reason, Roger doesn't seem to have a problem with his boys visiting the place. Vito runs most of his empire out of the Roxy: gambling, prostitution, the rackets. From what I hear, when the turf war ended, the two started being regulars at each other's places of business, and the Roxy has a rep as a good spot. Lots of legitimate people go there, so Roger must've felt like it was no big deal for Sammy to hang there in his time off. I would imagine he had a guy watching him though, just to be safe."

"You said he had a girl there?" Her hands were moving up my stomach now, expertly pushing and prodding my ligaments, my bone, and the torn fibers of my sinew.

"Yeah, Maxie. Except Maxie ain't a broad. He's a man, and it seems your husband's a Nancy." Her hands got rough at that, and I tensed. "You wanted to know so bad, I was trying to spare you."

"What else?" Her voice was very hard now. Her hands hovered over my abdomen. "I know you know something else. I can feel it."

"That's it, babe. I found out your old man's a fag, got shot at, and took off."

The mattress shifted with her weight and as it did a motorist below my window pulled a U-turn and bathed the room in a quick flash of light. Melanie was standing up straight on the bed, glaring down at me. She had on a leather get-up that looked to be straight out of a comic book. A glistening black leather corset ran the length of her abdomen, and cupped her breasts from beneath, pressing them up into the air but leaving them exposed. Her legs were covered in fishnet stockings that connected to the corset with small, lace ties. Her hair was down around her shoulders, and she was damn near the sexiest thing I had seen in the past few hours.

"Liar," she snarled. Before I knew what was happening she had punched me full on the jaw, snapping my head to the side. "You're lying! Who told you my husband was a fairy?"

"Everybody," I said, and grinned into the darkness, blood warm and coppery against my tongue. "It doesn't seem to be much of a secret."

"Liar!" she said again, and then dropped her full weight onto my face. My mouth, nose, jaw, everything was covered by her potent feminine scent and her short, curly, hair. I couldn't breathe save through her, which was a little difficult since she was grinding her hips into my face. Her thighs kept me in a headlock as she continued to gyrate, her voice sounding muffled as she spouted out orders, "Lick me, you beast, lick me until I set you free."

I did as I was told. Not because she ordered me to, I wasn't in the practice of taking orders from dames, but more because her lips were right there by mine and I'm a man and couldn't help myself.

She tasted sweet and I lapped the small mound above the lips, flicking it and nibbling on it. Her thighs closed harder against my ears, but I could feel the vibration of her ragged moans. At some point I became conscious that her weight had settled more firmly on my face, the hard rocking of her hips was rubbing my skin raw, and my lungs were beginning to burn from lack of oxygen. I'd just about made up my mind to play as rough as she was, making use of the only available weapon; my teeth. It was either that or suffocate, but just as I went to take a good, hard nip, she stood up again.

"You're plain nuts," I gasped. "You could've killed me!"

"I'm not done with you, yet." I could see her shadow above me, but her face was still bathed in darkness. "Who told you my husband was a fairy?" she asked again.

"Everybody," I repeated. "I'm telling you, it wasn't a big secret. Maxie is as fag as they come. He's little and squirrelly and not much of a man at all. If it makes you feel any better,

I think he's the one getting the full sodomy session, not Sammy."

"And where's Sammy?"

"I dunno." I shrugged against my restraints. "Nobody did. But I'll find out...."

She was on me again, but I had time to take a good breath as I felt the mattress shudder and her weight return to my face. I didn't need to be instructed this time. I probed her insides with my tongue and drank of her until she released me, gasping for air. She stood once more. In the flash of moonlight I could see her blue eyes and the fire smoldering behind them.

"Where is he?" she demanded again. "I know your type. You'll drag this out for weeks just to get the day-rate."

"Listen," I wheezed, "I'm being on the level with you here. I don't know. I asked, and I was real persuasive, but nobody knew. I'll find him, but it takes time."

"But he's alive?"

"I get the impression he is, sure."

She punched me again, leaned over and unsnapped something. The shadow moved from over me and returned to the floor and I felt a tug on my wrists and was led off the bed. She positioned me on my knees beside my bed, head bowed.

"You got that impression?"

"Yup."

"Why are you holding out on me?" she asked. "I want to know what's going on."

"Just as soon as I know, I'll let you in. Right now this is all I got." I looked up at her. "Don't act so surprised about the whole thing. There's a reason why you're getting tapped by Delaney and me. If Sammy was so good to you in that way, you wouldn't need other men. Right?"

"You don't tell me what I need," she spat. Literally. She spit right in my face, and then slapped me one good. "I think the lower social circle needs a lesson here."

"What?"

"I'm going to teach you a lesson. I pay you, you work for me. I don't care how much of a man you happen to be, you do what I say."

"Never gonna happen, babe." Even as I denied it, I knew that was exactly what I had been doing ever since she cuffed me, and realized I didn't mind the business all that much.

"Really?" She wrapped a collar around my neck and gave it a tug. It tightened like a choker on a Rottweiler. "I think we should work on that disobedient streak. What do you think?"

"I think if you get much more physical in a way I don't like, you're gonna have a real bad night once these cuffs come off."

She laughed at me, a deep, rolling laughter I hadn't expected from a dame. Then her foot touched my shoulder and I realized she was wearing boots. Not just any boots, but knee-high boots like I saw the paratroopers wearing during the war.

"Lick them," she said. "Lick my boots."

"What?"

"You heard me. You were in the service, right?"

"Sure."

"You know how to clean a pair of boots. I want my boots cleaned and I want it done with your tongue."

"You're one crazy ass broad, you know that?"

She said that she did and brought that big old boot right across my jaw. I spat blood onto my carpet, and touched my tongue to the smooth leather. Her head fell back and she laughed like a demon. I couldn't tell if her eyes were open but I made a bet that they weren't and rocked back on my heels. Before she had time to react, I sprang to my feet and made a grab for her throat, curling my fingers around her slender neck and bending her backwards as I squeezed. There was a sadistic satisfaction in hearing the air hiss from her lungs as I increased the pressure to her windpipe. In the faint glow of the moonlight, I could just make out the shock and horror in the same eyes that mocked me only moments before. Now," I growled, "I get to keep you from breathing until you answer *my* questions."

I released her just long enough so she could get a good, deep breath, and then clamped down even harder this time. I could see her exposed breasts in the moonlight, pale and glistening with sweat, rising and falling as she struggled to pry my fingers from around her throat. I allowed her another gulp of air, and then closed her windpipe again.

"Now," I said again, my mouth just inches from hers, "I wanna know some things. I wanna know why you have the number to Coronado's top lieutenant written in your matchbook. I wanna know why Roger Delaney is gunning for your old man. But most of all, I wanna know why I should believe anything other than my running theory, which is that you and Roger are working together to find Sammy and get him dead."

Even in the dim light I could see her skin turning blue. I shoved her away. She slammed up against the wall. I didn't feel all that bad about it either. While she was doubled over trying to catch her breath, I found the keys to my handcuffs and released myself. I was fuming, but couldn't seem to tear my eyes away from her heaving breasts as she gulped down air, couldn't seem to control how sexy she was. I was torn between strangling her with my bare hands and breaking her in half with a different part of my anatomy.

"Got some answers?" I asked finally.

"Go to hell, Glacier." she wheezed.

I was on her before she had a chance to move, or scream, or fight me off. My hands found her throat again and this time

I didn't let up. I tossed her onto the bed, my hands clasped tightly, my hips taking the brunt of her kicks and attempts to break free, and then I pressed myself against her. I felt her body tense as my manhood touched her thighs, and then she relaxed just a hair.

I let go of her throat, my fingers working their way down her chest to her breasts. She looked at me with glassy eyes for a moment, and then spit in my face again. I laughed at her, and kissed her hard on the mouth, our tongues working together and lashing out in anger at one another.

I entered her wetness with all the force of a man possessed, and she moaned and beat my chest with her fists. She dragged her nails along my skin, screaming in rage and trying to bite me, but even as she fought, her body welcomed the hostile invasion. Her hips thrust upward, meeting each punishing stroke, her inner heat spiking as her arousal grew stronger.

"Answer me!" I roared.

"Roger's taking over Coronado's turf," she ground out. She pulled my hair, took a swing at my face, then tried to gouge my eyes with her dangerous nails, but all the while she kept talking. "He wants Sammy out of the way, because he wouldn't go along."

"And Bob Vitorio? Coronado's man?" I asked, I could feel her straining under me, her muscles contracting, she was coming hard. "Where's he fit?"

"He'll take over the territory under Delaney. That's his reward for turning on his boss."

I erupted inside of her and she held me there, her face pressed to the side as the spasms continued to wrack her body. Feeling her climax sent a jolt of electricity surging through me, and I rode her through it until there was nothing left but the faint ripple of quivering muscles. I rolled away from her and stood up, watching her speculatively as she lay there motionless, sprawled across the rumpled sheets like a rag doll.

"I never loved him," she wouldn't look at me as she said it, "he forced me to marry him after the trial so I couldn't testify against him if he was indicted for perjury. He can't even get it up for a woman."

"Put on some decent clothes," I said in disgust, "and get out of my house. I'm off the case. You can keep your blood money." Then I left the room, went into the kitchen, poured myself a scotch and lit a smoke. She came out ten minutes later and walked past me without a word. She opened the door, pausing for a moment before turning around, her eyes begging me to understand.

"I never wanted any of this, Glacier," she said softly. "When Roger tells someone to do something, they do it, that's all."

"And when I say I'll do something, I do it," I told her. "And if I ever see you or Roger again, I'll kill the both of you."

(Continue to Chapter 10)

CHAPTER 9B

"Hey, babe." I said, lukewarm. "How's it going with you?"

"I've been waiting here for hours," she replied sourly. "What the hell happened? I need some answers. I've handed you a lot of money, Glacier, and not so you could go off and have a fun date night with your secretary."

"How'd you know about that?" I lit a smoke and leaned against the door jamb.

"I'm not a moron," she snarled. "Don't treat me like I'm stupid. I've got connections in this town, same as you."

"Really?" I mused. "What do you need me for then?"

"What did you find out at the Roxy?" She ignored my question. "I think I have a right to know."

"Okay," I nodded, "I'll tell you exactly what I know right now. I know your husband is either half, or all the way, a fag. I know that Big Roger Delaney has a hit out on him right now. I know who's got him, too. And I know you've been playing me the whole time."

It was then that she saw the Luger in my hand. The metallic sound as I flipped off the safety seemed to echo in the small room. In the glare of midnight New York, I could see her eyes go wide and glassy.

"What's that for?" she asked with a puff of smoke. "I'm your damn client!"

"Not anymore, sweet cheeks. Now you're just another scum bag I need to get information from." I took a long, slow drag off my smoke, and let it out in a cloud that temporarily obscured my face. "I got shot at tonight because of you and your queer ass husband."

"What?"

"Don't act surprised, kid, it doesn't become you to lie. I know you helped work it out. Maybe not the hit on me, but the one on your husband. Don't treat me like I'm stupid, either. I read your matchbook tonight. You've got Bob Vitorio's number written in it. Don't you think I know who that is?"

"That doesn't prove...."

"It proves you know Coronado's first lieutenant. And given the fact that Coronado's obviously nose deep in this, and that his boys shot at me tonight, and that I was told it was on his orders, and that Sammy hangs at the man's place, and that you're currently sleeping with Roger Delaney, and that Roger Delaney and Vito Coronado were five seconds away from re-igniting World-War-double-eye in the streets of New York just a year ago, that all adds up to proof enough for me. Enough proof to kick your ass outta my apartment, and maybe even enough to shoot you."

"You would never...."

"Don't make assumptions, lady. I'd do a lot of things you wouldn't expect."

"Well..." she stammered, "what do you want from me?"

"I want answers," I said, and pushed myself off the wall. "And I want them right now."

She stared at me as blank as a boarded up shop window, and I moved the barrel of the Luger towards the bedroom.

It still didn't register. Her eyes were glazed and her body completely motionless, her muscles so tense I thought they might break her bones. I motioned again and this time her head snapped back quickly and she shook it hard, trying to gain her bearings.

"What?" she asked.

"The bedroom. We're gonna talk in there."

"What..." her voice trailed off and her gaze slowly followed it toward the bedroom door, "what are you going to do to me?"

"Well," I cleared my throat and bit down on the smoldering butt of my smoke. The ashes were about to my lip, and I needed to get her moving soon or get a blister, "I figure you're my client, so I really shouldn't torture you... too bad. If I do it right, we might both have a good time before I cut you loose."

I pointed the Luger at her face, "Now move."

She did. She rose slowly from the chair and went, her movements mechanical as she walked to the bedroom. I followed at a safe distance behind, taking a moment to stamp out my Lucky in the ashtray before entering the bedroom and getting down to business.

"Now," I said, "go over to the drawer on the right side of the bed, open it up and take out my handcuffs."

"What?"

"Don't act like you didn't hear what I said, I don't like it when broads start acting smart with me."

She crossed the shadowy room and opened the drawer. I could hear the steel of the cuffs jingle in the darkness, caught a quick flash as the dim moonlight sparked off one of the chrome links.

"There's four pairs in here," she said, her voice low as a whisper, the whir of the fan nearly blowing her words away, "which one?"

"All of them."

"I'm not a damned convict, Glacier…"

"All of them." I put a nice snarl on the end so she'd know I was serious. She pulled them from the drawer and held them out to me. "Toss two of 'em on the bed," I said, "then cuff each wrist with a separate pair."

She shot me a curious glance but did as she was told.

I ordered her over to the radiator, a monstrous hunk of metal just opposite the bed, then told her to get down on her knees with her hands behind her back. Positioned as she was, submissive, her back to me, I decided she wasn't going anywhere and holstered my Luger. I could handle a dame like her with my hands anyway. She stayed put as I retrieved the other cuffs. Took the first pair and linked one end to the empty cuff on her left wrist then clipped the other end around her left ankle. I secured her right wrist to right ankle the same way, then maneuvered her around so she was facing me.

"Now," I said when I was done, "we talk." I pulled a switch-blade from my pocket. I could tell by her startled expression that Mrs. Marx knew what was hidden inside the handle. "But first," I triggered the slick mechanism that forced a seven inch stiletto out with a deadly click, "I think you should slip into something more comfortable."

Her dress was snug as a leather glove, clinging to her curves and making the journey of the blade a dangerous one as I slipped it beneath the cloth. I could feel her straining to hold back the quivers of fear as the blade nicked through the material at the hemline then continued up past her hips, dipping between her breasts, and slicing the last thin thread hugging her cleavage.

It took two swift flicks of the blade to sever her shoulder straps and send the dress slithering weightlessly to the floor.

All that remained was a lacy pair of black panties and matching brassiere. She didn't move. Didn't dare, not when the blade was hovering so close to her delicate skin.

"See now, that's better."

"You're an animal," she hissed.

"That won't get us off on the right path." I smiled through the darkness at her face, illuminated pale gray in the shifting moonlight. "I think that mouth would be better suited doing something else."

"Like what?" She looked down as she spoke, her voice so low it could barely be called a whisper.

"Answering my questions."

"Wha..." she shook her head, I watched as she shivered beneath the cool breeze of the fan. "What do you want me to tell you?"

"Roger," I said, "he put you up to this?"

"No..." she shivered again. I was beginning to think it wasn't from the breeze, "I wanted to find Sammy."

"I told you once not to lie." I crossed the room and got a bottle of bourbon from my sock drawer, poured myself a stiff one. "And now it's starting to frustrate me."

"I'm telling you the truth. I don't want Sammy to get hurt."

I took a long pull on my drink and walked back over to her, she shivered again as I approached. I looked down into her big eyes and for a moment I almost believed her. I set my drink on the bed and reached down, delving between her knees, moving my hand up along her thigh and touched her in her softest place. When I pulled my hand back it was moist and glistening, inviting, despite her protests.

"Having fun?" I asked.

"You're a bastard," she hissed.

"I want the truth, or I start to get rough."

"Roger..." she stammered, "Roger wants Sammy gone, but not so we can be together. He's trying to get rid of Coronado."

"And so he got in with the man's lieutenant?"

"Right. He hooked up with Bob, the guy on the matchbook, and they're going to work together."

"And Bob will get a nice chunk of territory under Delaney's control?"

"Right."

"Okay," I sighed. "How'd he hook up with Bob?"

"I... I was the go between."

"I see, so you have been to the Roxy before?"

"With Sammy."

"With Sammy," I mocked. I looked down at her. She was shaking with anticipation, waiting for me to touch her. She had never looked lovelier. I took a pull from my drink, placed it back on the bed, and knelt down in front of her.

"Now we can do this two ways," I told her, "the easy way or the hard way."

"What?"

"You can just spill it all from the beginning," I explained, "or you can do it between mouthfuls."

She looked at my crotch, at the tent pulsing there, and shuddered so hard her restraints clacked against each other.

"Hard," she said, swallowing.

"That's what I wanted to hear."

I stood and unzipped my pants, letting myself hang in her face. She eyed the tip and slowly flicked her tongue along her lips, wetting them in anticipation.

"Now," I arched my back a bit, growing closer and then pulling back, teasing her, "what does Sammy have to do with the war."

"I..." she shuddered again, her eyes wide and shimmering gray in the moonlight, "don't know."

I slid my member into her mouth and pressed forward with my hips, forcing the tip into her throat, she gagged reflexively for a moment, and then I felt her muscles relax as I fell into long, slow strokes. I grabbed a fist full of hair, thrusting in and out of her mouth and damn near losing it every time her lips slid along my shaft, making slurping noises. I had to hand it to the dame, she was taking it like a trooper, but I knew it was only a matter of time before she started choking on the saliva my pumping action was making.   It gushed from her mouth, dribbling down her chin and snaking a trail through the valley between her breasts soaking into her bra. When she started making meek little sounds of protest and straining against my grasp, I cut her some slack and pulled out, and started shouting at her.

"Answer me!"

The words flowed out of her like a flood.

"Sammy has the books.   Coronado needs them. If he can get his hands on them he'd be able to put Delaney behind bars. There wouldn't be a huge war, just a quiet takeover with Roger out of the way."

"Roger'd be dealt with inside then?"

She nodded vigorously, "It's cheaper that way, I guess."

"So Coronado made the first move?"

"I don't..."

Her mouth was full before she could finish.   This time I lodged myself so far down her throat, her nose was touching in my abdomen.   I held her there until she started to writhe, pulling out just long enough to let her take a gulp of air before forcing her to swallow every last inch of me.   There were no tell tale signs she was going to pass out, save the slight flutter of her eyelashes, but I figured she couldn't be getting even a whisper of air with me jammed halfway down her windpipe. I yanked her head back, waiting impatiently for her coughing fit to subside, then pushed my way past her reluctant lips once more. She let out a frightened squeak but settled down fast enough when I steadied into an unhurried pace, gliding in and out of her lovely mouth until my balls were so tight I had to pull out or risk shooting off the fireworks too soon.

"Did he, or didn't he?"

"He didn't," she gasped. She swallowed a few times so she could talk without drooling, while I entertained myself by following the damp path that now extended past her bra, down her glistening stomach, and beyond the lacy band of her panties. "Delaney had the whole thing planned, but Sammy made his move. He went to Coronado and spilled it all, and Vito figured the easy way out would be to snatch up Sammy and make him comfortable, then make his move while Roger was off balance."

"How do you know all this?"

"I'm sleeping with Roger, remember?"

"But Sammy running off makes you look bad too, right? So you figure you'll track the bastard down and turn him in yourself, that way you'd be cleared?"

"No, I'd never turn on Sammy."

"Liar!"

Gripping her by the back of the neck, I forced her face down to the ground, held her there while I used the blade to snip the thin band of her panties, then retracted it again. She tried to wriggle away, but I held her firmly in place. With her rear jutting in the air, exposing her most vulnerable parts, I gripped her hips and shoved into her heated opening, mercilessly pounding the lovely Melanie Marx until she couldn't take it anymore.

"Sammy's queer!" she screamed as I came inside her. "We've never even made love."

I dropped my hold on her hips, my compassion only mildly stirred when she dropped to the floor, cracking her hip bones on the hardwood. I went to the bed and retrieved my drink, sucking it down in between gulps of air.

"I know that," I said as I slowly got my wits back, "I told you that earlier."

"He…" she was gasping for air, fighting the cuffs, but not to escape, rather so she could lay flat against the passing ecstasy. "He made me marry him. After the trial, the cops were going to indict him and use me as a witness. He forced me to marry him so I couldn't testify."

I set the empty glass on the nightstand and dragged my pants back up. Took my time fastening my belt, then, after what must have felt to her like an eternity, I unlocked the restraints and laid them back in the drawer.

"I'm off the case," I told her. "You can keep your damned blood money. I don't want to see or hear anything from you or Roger ever again. I'm gonna step out for some more bourbon, and when I get back you'd best be gone. Because if not, I swear to god I'll put a bullet in you and your damn boss."

With that, I left my apartment, and prayed I never saw that dame again.

(Continue to Chapter 10)

CHAPTER 9C

I ignored the woman sitting at my table and went straight to my bedroom.

"Glacier!" I heard her growl from the other room, but ignored the voice.

I shut the door behind me and headed for the bathroom. Shut that door, too. Washed my face, doused a little water under my armpits and dried off , then went back out again. Crawled into bed and pulled the covers high. I didn't want anything to do with the broad at the moment. There was too much going on and too much I didn't get. I thought I saw the whole thing taking shape, but with my eyelids as droopy as they were, I couldn't make out any definite lines.

Before I knew it, the gray walls had turned black and I was deep in sleep.

I woke when a supernova exploded under my eyelids. I rolled out of the bed and landed on the floorboards with a hard *thunk*. Three guys were standing over me and the one with the sap was leering at me. The lights were on, and it took a moment for my eyes to adjust, but his body language did the talking before I could even see his face. When it came into focus I knew who I was looking at.

"Jesus H Christ!" I mumbled. "Roger, the hell are you doing here?"

"Where is he, Glacier?"

"Who?"

"Sammy, where's Sammy?"

"I don't know," I was stalling, trying to think my way out of it. My piece was hanging in the shoulder holster on my bed post, the wrong one; I would have to climb over the bed to get to it. When I turned my head to gauge the distance, another burst of lights went off in my head. Roger had hit me with the damned sap while I was stone cold asleep. A cowardly thing to do, but I knew it wasn't beneath him. He was the type of man who wouldn't let his boys have all the fun, and smart enough not to take any chances on me while I was awake.

"I haven't found out yet," I told him.

"You're a bum of a private eye just like you were a bum as a cop and a soldier before that." Roger leaned back and handed the sap to one of his men. The empty hand was quickly filled with a snub-nosed revolver.

"Come on, Glacier, where's he at?"

"Who told you I knew anything about where he was?"

"That," he grinned, "pretty much tells me you do." He rolled his shoulders for effect. "Tell you what I'm gonna do for you, Glacier, cuz we've know each other so long. I'm gonna make this an easy decision. Either you tell me now," he cocked the hammer and pointed the stubby barrel at my groin, "or I blow your little prick off."

(You know what? I'm just going to stop this right here. I don't want poor Glacier to have to suffer for your incompetence. "Go to bed." That's the answer? Do you live your whole life like that? Just run away from your problems, that'll help. You've got a sexy dame in your kitchen and your response is to breeze right past her and fall asleep? I mean, we all need our rest, but it was pretty damned obvious she was in on it after the shooting and the interrogations. *sigh* I'm going to give you one more chance, go back and try again, and man up while you're at it. Because just like when you found the diaphragm in your wife's purse after your vasectomy, you may not want to think about it, but you sure as shit have to eventually.)

CHAPTER 10

There was a bird I didn't recognize squawking in my right ear as I opened my eyes. It took me a moment to focus, but when I had, I realized first that the sun was shinning through my window from a high angle, which meant it was well past noon. The second thing was that the squawking wasn't a bird, but rather my phone incessantly ringing like the person on the other end had nothing else to do with their life but hang on until I answered.

I let it ring a few more times for good measure than grabbed it off the hook.

"Glacier," I croaked. I needed coffee and a cigarette. Bourbon might be nice as well.

"Glacier..."

"No, that's my name."

"I know that," Hugo huffed, "that's why I'm calling you."

"To remind me? Well, thanks." I hung up.

Hugo McEachern was my oldest friend. I met him in boot camp, and we had served together through most of the war. Watched him bed a fair number of fräuleins and he'd seen me do the same. When we got out, we both joined the force together. Walked the beat together. Made it to detectives together. Always together.

He had done everything but hang on to my ankles to stop me from going into the private field, but had failed. This was the first we had spoken since I walked out of the precinct a free man. There were only two reasons for him to call: he needed something or he knew something. I guessed it could also have something to do with the dead bodies from the Roxy, but I doubted it.

The phone rang again, I answered it.

"Glacier..." Hugo began.

"Are we gonna do this all over again?"

"Stop being smart and listen."

"Listening."

"You working for Missus Marx?"

"Not anymore. Why?"

"When'd you stop working for her?"

"About..." I tried to remember. "Sometime very early this morning."

"Well," I heard him take a short breath, "maybe that's for the best, then."

"Why?"

"We just caught up with her."

"Was she running from someone?"

"Apparently," he grumbled, "and whoever it was, they found her and did the job they were looking to do."

I knew what that meant. I had three choices in a situation like this.

A. Tell Hugo it's not your problem, hang up and go back to sleep. - flip to Chapter 11a.

B. Tell Hugo you'll be there in ten minutes and take off right away. No shower, no shave, just get there. - flip to Chapter 11b.

C. Tell Hugo you'll be there in twenty. Shower, shave, then pick up smokes and coffee on the way. - flip to Chapter 11c.

CHAPTER 11A

"That's really not my problem, ol' buddy," I told him. "I quit on her, and I have a feeling whatever she got, she deserved."

"But Glacier...."

"Nope," I said as I sat up, "I'm done. Thanks for thinking of me though, and give me a call later this week, we'll have drinks."

"Fine, Glacier, if that's how you want it."

"It is." I hung up again.

I let my head hit the pillow and started thinking. That was the last thing I wanted to do. I wanted to sleep. But I couldn't keep my mind from roaming.

I didn't feel the least bit sorry about Mrs. Marx getting axed. People die in New York all the time. Every single day someone gets gunned down, mugged, burned up, something. And she played with a bad crowd. Anyone could have seen her life was going to end in an untimely manner. She had set up her old man, lied and used me, and been willing to be a part of a mob war. What did she expect to happen?

I got up and made myself some coffee, then hit the shower and shaved, pulled on my coat and went out the door. The coffee had finished brewing but I left it there, it would be warm enough when I got back. I hit the streets and made my way towards my favorite deli, the place where they make the real New York breakfast: lots of meat and eggs and cheese on a bagel. My mouth was watering before I made it ten paces.

I flipped a cigarette in my mouth and started thinking about my breakfast. Hot coffee and a good meal. That would start my day off right.

Day, well, afternoon was more accurate, I guessed.

I had my rent paid and a little extra in my pocket. That would get me by until another blonde walked through my door. And I was pretty certain that when your client is executed in a gangland murder, it severs any previous contractual arrangements.

There was a scuffle behind me, and I turned, trailing smoke, and saw two wops standing tall on the sidewalk, holding pistols and pointing them at me.

"Mister Delaney says hi." One of them said. I was trying to figure out why these guys were there, interrupting my dreams of breakfast, and not really listening to what he said. It registered in my brain just as the cracks of gunfire erupted in my eardrums.

The first hit me high in the chest, and spun me around like a dreidel. Then two more pounded into me, one in my spine and the second in my throat. I felt a hot mist spray from my exposed artery and watched as my blood splattered on the hard wall beside me, the bright red beginning to pool and run down to the ground even as I spun ever further around. I came full circle and saw my attackers once more, just as they released their second volley.

I hit the ground, my head slapping against the pavement so hard it recoiled and bounced a few times. My hands went numb, then my face, finally everything became coated with fuzzy splinters and my vision went black.

(Jesus! I'm starting to think you get off on this! Is that what it is? You like watching people get hurt? Huh, tough guy? How about I let Glacier go over to your house and see who's the better man? I can't believe this! I let you have control, and you bitch out when a dame's just been murdered? Glacier's a man's man. He's not just going to let somebody take out a broad he's been laying it to for a hundred pages! He's gonna make someone pay, and that's just what you're going to do: go back, choose again, and make it count. I want to see blood-shed God damn it!)

CHAPTER 11B

"I'll be there in ten." I hung up, didn't wait for a reply.

My head was still foggy but I decided to forgo the shower and the coffee. I pulled on my clothes, lit a smoke, and had a nip of bourbon for breakfast. Then headed out the door. Came back and pulled on my shoes. Out again.

The precinct was close, only about three blocks, so I decided to walk it rather than take a cab. I had promised to be there in ten, and the cab ride would've taken twenty. I made it in five walking.

The boys at the counter ignored me as I passed them and made my way upstairs. I didn't think they remembered me, but I didn't think they felt like getting up to chase me down, either.

Hugo was at his desk, holding his head in the catcher's mitt he called a hand. He didn't rise when I walked up, and didn't look at me when I sat down.

"So," I began, "somebody smoked the little lady."

"Yup," he dropped his hand and looked into my eyes. He had a bulldog face and ears like flap jacks, not an attractive man and his wife was less so. She was less attractive than Hugo, that is, but also less of a man. "Put three bullets in her head."

"All three? Seems like one would of done."

"Probably," he sighed.

"I quit her late last night, early this morning," I told him.

"Why?"

"Didn't like the job anymore." I lit a smoke. "She hired me to find her old man, but I didn't think he really wanted to be found."

"What's he into?"

"You know what he's into."

"Sure," he sighed, "but what's he into?"

"Mob banking."

"And?" He slammed a hand on his desk. "That got him killed?"

"I never said he was dead, I said he didn't want to be found. I don't think dead men care one way or the other."

"Glacier, I need to know what I'm up against."

"I'll let you know when I know, but I need some help."

"Like what?"

I told him.

"Glacier, my friend, I can't do that."

"Yes you can. Come on, for old time's sake."

He studied me. "Fine, fine, fine," he finally said. "But if you make a great big mess, I'm gonna hear about it."

"It'll be cleaner my way than the other," I told him, clapped him on the back and went out the way I'd come in.

I knew what I needed to do. I just didn't know how to go about doing it. So I had breakfast at a corner deli to mull it over while I ate. Sausage, bacon, eggs, cheese, hash browns, all on an everything bagel. When the waitress asked me what I'd like to drink, I winked at her.

"Gin and tonic please," I said.

"What are you some kinda health nut?"

"And coffee."

That seemed to make her feel better.

The food came and went, and I sat sipping my gin and looking out the window. I kept replaying the events of the last night over in my mind. Telling Mrs. Marx to keep her blood money. Threatening to kill her if I ever saw her again. Screwing the hell out of her.

I thought I had all the pieces of the puzzle. The only thing I didn't know was who had pulled the trigger on the dame. That was the most important point. Who did the real killing? Whoever had punched Mrs. Marx's card was the real one to worry about. The other could wait.

The pieces floated around inside my head, jumbled and out of focus at first, but eventually they started to fall into place. Sammy, Melanie, Roger, and Vito. All gunning for the same piece of the pie. All twisted in the same little scheme, playing each other in their own little ways.

I got up, paid the bill, and made my way home. When I got in, I put on a pot of coffee, smoked a Lucky in the shower, shaved and put on my best suit and hat. Then I loaded my Luger and went out into the kitchen.

As I poured myself a highball, there was a knock, and I answered it with my Luger in my hand.

"Package, sir," the messenger said.

"Thanks," I took it and tipped him a half-dollar.

"Wow, thanks Mister Glacier."

I set the heavy package on the table, looked at it. Left it there and went out. Came back in. Took the pot of coffee off the stove. Sucked down my highball. Went back out.

I decided to walk to the office to clear my head. It was swirling now with all the events of the previous few days. Too many things going on at once. Most of them involving me inside some dame I barely knew. Those ones were pretty clear.

I trotted up the stairs to my office, images of my last encounter with Missus Marx running through my head on an endless loop. It was starting to hurt. If I thought too much about her my pants started getting tight, and then I remembered she was dead and I got angry and wanted revenge.

I walked through the door, sighed, and tossed my coat onto the chair. It didn't land right. Probably because there was a dame sitting in it.

Mrs. Marx.

Only younger than the last time I had seen her. By about five years. This Mrs. Marx was in her early twenties, even more beautiful, and looking at me with misty eyes.

"Mister Glacier?"

"That's what it says on the door."

"But you are *the* Rick Glacier?"

"You asked me that last time," I said.

"Excuse me?"

I studied her for a moment. This wasn't Melanie Marx, unless she had un-shot herself and gotten a lot younger. I thought dead women didn't *lose* a few years when they got resurrected, so odds were good she was a relative.

"Who are you?" I asked.

"I'm Samantha Brooks," she explained, "Melanie was my older sister."

Bingo.

"I'm sorry for your loss," was all I could think of to say.

"Thank you," she nodded. "What are you going to do about it?"

I hesitated. This was a serious question. If I answered it wrong it could blow up in my face, big time. I needed her. Well, I wanted her. And I wasn't about to pass up a fling with the sister of a dame I'd laid it to. I'd never done that. Not once.

"I'm going to kill some people," I said.

"How many people?"

"More than one, less than a hundred."

"That's a wide margin," she raised a perfect eyebrow.

"Just being honest," I told her.

She shifted slightly, and put a tiny hand into her purse, then extracted a cigarette case, flipped it open, and took out two perfectly rolled smokes. She lit one and handed it to me.

"I knew I could count on you," she said.

I took the cigarette from her, put it between my lips and took a hard pull, drawing the expensive smoke into my lungs. It was strong. I liked it.

"How will you go about doing it?" she asked softly. "I mean, finding the people responsible."

"A man like me has resources, kid, people who tell me things."

"A man like you," her voice was even softer now, her tongue playing with her lower lip, "knows how to ask the right questions, I'd imagine."

I tossed my smoke, pulled her into my arms and kissed her hard on the mouth. She took it, gave it back, and before I knew it my shirt had joined my coat on the floor. We kissed again, her tongue probing me like she expected to find gold hidden behind my tonsils.

Her dressed dropped weightlessly to her ankles, revealing nothing but bare skin and she attacked my pants like they were an enemy she needed to dispose of as quickly as possible, yanking them down so I could step out of them.

I leaned back, propping myself against the desk then cupped her shapely bottom and hoisted her up, growing hard as rock when she anchored her legs around my hips. I teased her with the tip of my shaft for a few minutes before driving myself all the way inside of her. She let out a wild gasp, her eyes glazing over as I guided her up and down with a long, leisurely strokes. I had every intention of making this exceptionally pleasurable encounter last for a good solid hour or two, but the fire was already licking through my veins, quickly burning out of control. Apparently, she thought so too. She drew her arms up over her head and arched backwards until her head was almost touching the floor, the movement as graceful as it was arousing. I kept a firm grip on her hips, let her sink a little lower so that the back of her shoulders were braced against the floor, then proceeded to drill her like a jackhammer.

She felt incredible, her throaty moans exciting me and spurring me on until I was pounding into her so hard and fast that the features of her face and those glorious, bouncing breasts were little more than a blur. I felt a surge and pulled out at the last second, showering my seed over her stomach and breasts.

I gently lowered her to the floor, took a smoke out of her container and lit it. Lit another and handed it to her where she lay, panting on the asbestos.

"My God," she whispered.

"It wasn't God, babe," I told her. "It was all Rick Glacier."

I left her there, quickly put on my clothes and headed out. Called over my shoulder that I'd let her know when I found something. I had no way of reaching her and felt no need to ask, confident that she would find me for round two.

I had a decision to make. I needed answers. I needed to talk to someone on the street who knew what was happening. I had three good contacts that would have my answers, but I only needed to talk to one.

A. Talk to Janet Melvue, Madam and long time Delaney squeeze. - flip to Chapter 12a.

B. Talk to Beatrice Little, mob dame and owner of the Lucky Six club and casino. - flip to Chapter 12b.

C. Talk to John Blonton, a femme and vet that now worked as a gay call-boy. - flip to Chapter 12c.

CHAPTER 11C

"I'll be there in twenty," I told Hugo. Hung up without listening to the reply.

I needed to move. I sprinted through the shower, hopped out and toweled off and then drew a razor across my face, leaving blood trickling down in odd angles. Chugged down some corn whiskey to kill the morning breath.

I was out the door.

Halfway to the precinct I stopped in a deli, bought a pack of Lucky's, a book of matches and a pot of coffee. Literally. The whole pot. Tossed the lady a buck and told her to buy herself a new one. It was half empty by the time I got there and I gave it to a bum sitting out front. Went inside.

The place was hopping like it always was. Whores and pimps and blacks all lined up in cuffs, waiting to be processed. I nodded to the boys behind the front desk and went past them, up the stairs to Hugo's office.

Hugo looked like what he was: inbred southern white trash. Two saucers for ears, and a face that only a mother could love. A mother and his wife, who was about as attractive as a Bulldog in heat.

"Jesus Glacier," Hugo said as greeting, "what have you got me into now?"

"Nothing I can't get myself out of," I told him.

"You were working for Missus Marx." It wasn't a question.

"Until last night, early this morning."

"Why'd you quit her?"

"Didn't like the job anymore."

"Why?" he snarled. Hugo was a good cop, but he would always be a cop, and he didn't like paperwork. We both knew one way or the other, this case would be generating the stuff in heaps.

"She hired me to find her husband," I explained. "I didn't think he wanted to be found."

"What's he into?" Hugo pulled a bottle of bourbon from his desk drawer and poured us each three fingers worth.

"Same as always," I told him, gulped down the firewater. "Except now he's MIA."

"Right," I set the glass down, "but I'll find him, and whoever popped the lady."

"Now Glacier," he scowled, wiped his face with a giant, meaty palm, "the DA will have my ass, I let you make a mess."

"It'll be cleaner my way," I said. "And you've got plenty of ass to spare."

We looked at each other.

"Fine," he sighed, "what do you need from me?"

I told him.

"Now, Rick," he cautioned, "that's something I can't do for you."

"Have to," I said, "boys I'm going up against, I'll need all the help I can get."

He looked around, drew the last of the bourbon past his lips, set down the glass and leaned in close.

"Fine, but you keep my name out of it."

"You're the best, McEachern."

I got up and went out the same way I came in. Past the blacks and crooks, and hit the street at a fast walk. The hobo was gingerly trying to mend his burnt hands from where I had tossed the hot pot of coffee into them. I reminded him to use the handle next time.

Five minutes later I was back at my apartment, mounting the steps three at a time. Five stories up I started to get winded and decided to have a smoke as I went. At the landing I stopped and stared. Carlene was standing in front of my door, crying softly.

I opened it up and let her inside. She looked like she'd cried about all the water out of her, so I made us each a stiff highball and downed them both while she collected herself.

"What's the matter, babe?" I asked when she was ready.

"That woman you were working for," she explained, "I heard she was killed last night."

"Last night, early this morning."

"That's just awful!" she moaned. "What happened?"

"Whatever she was into, it caught up with her."

"But I was with you last night, when we…" She shuddered.

"Whoa there, babe, don't think like that." I wrapped my arms around her and pulled her in close. "Nothing's going to happen to you."

"How do you know?" she mumbled into my chest.

"Because they would have to go through me to get to you," I told her. "Do I look like a man you can get through?"

She drew herself back and sized me up, but it wasn't for a fresh shirt.

"No," she said softly.

I pulled her chin up with the tips of my fingers, and kissed her on the mouth, savoring the taste of her tongue on mine. She tasted like lemon water, or what I imagined lemon water must taste like to the sissies that drank it.

I let her unbutton my shirt, slowly, sensually, and rub her palms over the rippling muscles of my torso. Her hands were soft as they touched me, and I felt something else grow hard. My fingers ran through her hair and she lowered herself to her knees and unclasped my belt, then pulled the zipper and tugged my pants down.

She went slow, playfully working the balls and the shaft with her fingers as she stuffed the tip into her mouth. I was too big and long to get much more than that in, but she did her best, and when I'd had enough, I scooped her up in my arms and laid her out on the table like a Thanksgiving feast.

I could hear her breath coming out in short little gasps as I slowly inched her dress up past her waist then spread her legs. I was pleasantly surprised to discover she wasn't wearing any panties, not that it would have taken much to get them off her, but I was eager to taste the tender flesh that was glistening so invitingly before me. I laid a moist trail of kisses along the inside of her thighs then got to the main course and dove in. My tongue swirled inside of her, flicking upward now and then to tease the sensitive nub, careful to keep her teetering on the edge but denying her the release she was begging me for. I worked her over good, kept her legs spread wide so she was fully exposed, kissing and sucking and licking her raw until she was practically in tears. Only then did I slip my finger inside her, easily locating the engorged spot I knew would send her soaring, and gently applied pressure.

It was like having your face pressed to the ground when the sprinkler system went off, except the juices spurting out of Carlene were warm and sweet as honey.

I stood up, wiped my face off with a towel and looked at her. Her beautiful skin was flushed and she seemed to be about done, but I wasn't finished with her yet. I entered her slowly, stretching her inner muscles inch by inch until I'd buried the full fourteen inside her hot little body. Her eyes widened, lips parting as a low moan vibrated in the back of her throat. I took my time, moving in and out of her in long, measured strokes. Occasionally positioned her legs over my shoulders or turning Carlene onto her stomach and entering her from behind.

I didn't break any records for stamina, but did manage to hold off the big bang for the better part of two hours. Pretty impressive, considering she was tighter than baseball stitching and I had things to do. Pure perfection, Carlene was. It was a shame to let the pleasure end, but far too agonizing to hang on any longer. After draining what felt like every last once of bodily fluid, I stumbled back and sat down. Lit a smoke.

"Feel better?" I croaked.

"Mmmmnph," she moaned, "much better."

There was a knock at the door. I answered it. The delivery boy's mouth dropped as he looked at Carlene, then at me, and then down at the rod between my legs.

"P-p-package for Mister Glacier," he stammered.

"Well, what do you want? A kiss?" I tore the package out of his hands and slammed the door. Went back to the table and dropped it with a thud next to Carlene.

It was time to move.

"When you're ready, babe, get dressed, make yourself a drink and a bite to eat if you want, I got work to do."

"What are you going to do?" she asked. "About the lady."

"I'm going to kill some people."

"Really?"

"A lot of people," I said. Pulled on my pants, fastened my belt, and put on my shirt. "I hate to leave you like this, but I don't have much choice."

"It's alright, Rick," she cooed, "go do your job."

I went out knowing I had a decision to make. I needed to find out who axed Mrs. Marx, and I needed to know right now. There were three people I knew that would have the answer, but I only needed to talk to one.

A. Talk to Janet Melvue, Madam and long time Delaney squeeze. - flip to Chapter 12a.

B. Talk to Beatrice Little, mob dame and owner of the Lucky Six club and casino. - flip to Chapter 12b.

C. Talk to John Blonton, a femme and vet that now worked as a gay call-boy. - flip to Chapter 12c.

CHAPTER 12A

I decided to talk with Janet Melvue, a former whore turned madam. She had also spent about five years on the arm of Roger Delaney. He still came to see her now and again, because unlike pimps she kept her girls clean and off the hooch. She didn't hit her girls, and she didn't let the Johns do it either. All in all, she got about an ounce of gold worth out of each hour with one of her ladies, and they gave a good service to make it worth your while.

I stopped by a pawn shop and picked out a ten dollar ring from a Jew with numbers on his arm. Reminded him I was one of the boys kept him from getting gassed, and he dropped the price to eight.

One thing about Madam Melvue was she always liked to get gifts. Especially if you wanted information. She wasn't the kind of broad you roughed up to get the goods, not unless she asked you to.

The brothel was on the top floor of a new Manhattan building, the kind they pieced up with those Indians not afraid of heights. Big tall steel building, covered with brick so as to make it look like it belonged there. There was a colored man at the door, who smiled and opened it for me. I dropped him a quarter and he nodded appreciatively. There was a colored man in the elevator, who asked me for the floor, smiled knowingly when I told him the top floor, and brought me up. I gave him a half dollar and he wished me a good day.

I made a mental note to avoid any more black fellows. I was running out of change.

A mick the size of a refrigerated truck stopped me at the door. He wasn't looking for a tip, he was looking for a piece, and he found one strapped under my arm. I told him the Madam wouldn't mind, he disagreed, and I gave up. Let him hold on to it while I went in. He didn't ask if I was a cop, because he didn't really care one way or the other.

The place was all decked out in soft colors and hard surfaces. Lots of wood. Thick oak, mahogany; the type of stuff you buy when you're charging ten bucks an hour for a good time.

A little wop took my coat, and I wondered if they were breeding minorities in the place, with all the extra help they had, but didn't have time to decide before Madam Melvue stepped out of a side door, looked at me, and sighed.

"Rick Glacier," she said, "as I live and breathe."

"Madam Melvue," I smiled, "looking as amazing as ever."

And she did look amazing. Long, flowing brown hair down to the small of her back. A long red dress that dragged across the marble floor with two kids trying to hold it up as she walked. She had jewelry covering every spot she could fit it. Neck, ears, wrists, all gold and glittering with diamonds. Her face was long and lean, her body perfectly curved, breasts large and pushing at the top of her plunging neckline.

"Oh, yes," she feigned modesty, "flattery is certainly one way to a woman's heart."

"Here's another," I said, handing her the small box containing the ring.

"Oh Rick," she smiled, "you shouldn't have."

She tossed the box to one of the children without opening it.

"But you're not here to shower me with gifts, what can I do for you?"

"I need to talk about a client of mine," I told her.

"What kind of client?" She cocked one long, thin, penciled eyebrow.

"The dead kind."

She giggled, looked at me and thought better of it, covered her mouth with a tiny, perfect little hand. "Oh Rick Glacier," she scolded, "did you go and get one of your clients killed? That's not very professional."

"Can we talk somewhere," I asked, "more private?"

She looked around, as though startled we were out in the open, standing in the foyer. She wasn't, of course, because we were alone save for the kids holding her dress tail. Then she smiled at me again, and nodded, leading me through the door she had exited.

It was a bedroom, as they all were, and luxuriously decorated with plush cushioned chairs, fancy paintings, and a thick, soft bed. She sat on it, and lit a smoke with a gold lighter.

"So, Glacier, what have you gotten yourself into now?"

I took the smoke she offered, and sat down heavily in one of her chairs.

"A mob war is what it looks like," I said. "Looks like I'm right in the middle of Delaney and Coronado."

"That is not a very pleasant place to be," she winked. "It could get you in all kinds of trouble."

"It's already gotten me into the worst kind," I growled. "Murder, woman. Somebody shot my client, I want to know who."

"And that's why you're here?" She raised that eyebrow again. "To find out who killed her?"

"That's about the gist of it," I nodded, "yeah."

"And why do you think I know the answer to this incredibly dark question?" She puffed daintily on her cigarette, blowing the smoke in my face.

"Because whoever did it, odds are they do business here. And because you know everything that goes on in the streets."

"Oh yes," she sighed, "*of course* I do." She looked around, breathless, waving a hand to cool herself off. "But why should I give *you* such valuable information? It would almost certainly result in more bloodshed. Correct?"

"Because of my winning personality, for starters," I said. "And because I'll have to take it from you if you don't."

"Well," she sighed again. "Mister Glacier, I'm afraid that's exactly what you will have to do."

I stood then, took two steps, closing the gap, and laid one on her cheek with the back of my hand. Her whole body moved with the force of the blow, and she stayed with her head bowed for a few moments. Then she sat back up, smiled through bloody lips, and kicked straight up between my legs. I doubled over and she punched me square in the jaw. It was a good solid hit, from the shoulder, but not enough.

I grabbed a handful of her hair and used it to pull her out of the chair, dragged her over to the bed and tossed her there, writhing around, trying to hit me, missing because she couldn't see through the long hair. I flipped her over onto her stomach, undid my zipper and let her feel the full, hard length of it through the fabric of her dress.

"Now, what were you saying?"

"Nothing," she spat. "I'm not telling you nothing!"

"That's what I hoped you'd say."

I pulled up her dress and entered her from behind, yanking back her hair to arch her back. I didn't go easy on her; let her have all fourteen inches right out of the gate. She could take it, and did. I pounded her again and again, drawing all the way out and slamming back in. Hard. Brutal. Punishing.

She screamed and tried to fight me off, but I was in her and I wasn't pulling out any time soon. I pounded harder, faster, my hips slapping her buttocks, my hand pulling her hair until I thought it might come out, then shoved her face back down onto the mattress.

"You'll have to do better than that!" she screamed into the thick, flowery bedspread.

I did. I pulled out for a moment, moved up slightly, and dove into the other hole. I'd been in a lot of tight spots but she took the grade. She tried to squirm away from me, screaming, clawing at the sheets, but I kept at it.

I couldn't let her off that easy.

She needed to know I meant business, needed answers, and I was willing to break her in half to get them. I dove in as far as I could go, grabbed another handful of hair, pulled it back hard, and settled into a rhythm. As soon as I felt her start to loosen up, I started pumping harder, faster, giving her hair a tug for good measure. Her head was twisted at an almost obscene angle in an attempt to keep me from yanking her hair out by the roots. I gave her something else to worry about. A strangled sob tore from her throat when I forced the last four inches in, pulled her head up close to mine, and whispered in her ear.

"I'm gonna snap you in two, got that?"

Her eyes widened, fear flickering across her face when I loosened my grip on her hair and drew my hips back. I'd seen that same look in the eyes of a gangster as he stared down the barrel of my Lugar. I let her sweat it out for a second then plunged back in. Her head fell forward, her muffled moans keeping time with each thrust. I kept the pace steady, enjoyed watching myself slide in and out, and the sensation that shot through me each time her muscles clamped down in response. But like all good things, it had to end. I let her have it all, full throttle, held nothing back. Madam Melvue wasn't the only one grunting and violently shuddering as the rush of liquid heat shot up inside of her then slowly drained out and slipped between the crevices of her swollen lips.

I sat back down in the chair and knocked a Lucky out of my pack, sparked it with a match and eyed her.

"Now," I panted, "are you gonna tell me what I want to know, or do we need to go another round?"

"It was Delaney," she said softly, out of breath. "He doesn't care about Sammy anymore. He's moving on Coronado tonight."

"When?"

"I don't know," she sighed, tried to move, decided better of it. My eyes followed the deposit I'd made slowly wind its way down her leg. "No one knows. He just said 'it's time to move' and all his guys left with him."

"How long ago?"

"About an hour, maybe two. I'm not thinking real clear right now."

"Where is he?"

"What?" She looked up, a faraway look in her eyes.

"Where is he?" I asked again.

"At the bar." She settled back onto the covers. "The Joint. He'll have his men holed up in there until they move."

I pushed myself out of the chair and yanked my pants up, tucking my shirt back in before zipping the fly and straightening my jacket. Madam Melvue watched me dress. She looked perfectly at peace, content as kitten. Guess she liked where she was, in a position of submission, my seed dripping from her backside.

"Comfy?" I asked.

"Never been better," she laughed.

I turned to go.

"Glacier," she said. I turned. "Go get 'em."

I would. But I needed my package first. Would they keep until I went home and made it all the way to Brooklyn? I had a decision to make.

A. Go home and get the package, then go after Delaney and his boys. - flip to Chapter 13a.

B. Go straight there, to hell with the package, kill Delaney with your bare hands if necessary. - flip to Chapter 13b.

CHAPTER 12B

I decided to hit up Beatrice Little at her club and casino, the Lucky Six. I always thought she should've known the lucky number was seven, but I didn't have the heart to tell her. Maybe she knew and was just trying to be different, or maybe Lucky Seven was taken. Either way the club's name remained the same.

I took a cab. Then the subway, then walked a bit for the air. The sun was setting and it was cooling off. Lights would soon be on all over the city. The Lucky Six would be heating up when I got there, not that it ever cooled down.

Beats had bought the place, at that time a bar, and remodeled it. She set up an upscale club and a back room with every type of gambling known to man. Cops and politicians got in for free, a couple chips on the house, and that was all that was needed to keep her in business. That and having them owe her huge sums of money when her crooked games took every penny they had.

I went in and found a bully named Mo behind the bar. He had a handlebar mustache he curled at the ends, just a bit, to make him look like an Italian boxer. I never liked the man.

"Whatchu want, Glacier?" he snarled through his whiskers. "We don't take no Dicks in here."

I knew Beats would, but decided not to press the point. "I want to talk to the Beats," I told him.

"Beats don't wanna talk with you," he said, walked away.

I followed him to the end of the bar, pushed a patron out of the way and reached across the counter. I pinched his mustache between two of my thick fingers, and pulled. He yelped like a small dog being kicked, and I drew close to his ear.

"Beats want to talk yet?"

"Yeah, yeah I think she might," he grumbled. "Lemme go check."

I let him go and he disappeared around the corner. The patron I had pushed away stared at me. He was a squirrel of a man, nothing much at all, and I pushed him again for being a pansy. He cried out and scampered away. I saluted him with the drink he'd left behind. Downed it in one gulp. Lit a smoke.

The place was darkly lit, with booths running along all four walls, only split by the bar and two doors; one an exit, and one leading to the back rooms and the action. There was another door behind the bar that Mo guarded, two thugs guarded the others.

"Well, well, well," Beats said as she emerged from the bar door. I swiveled around in my chair to take her in. She was tall, thin, with black hair and piercing black eyes. She had been some kind of Indian back before becoming a New Yorker, and she always took my breath away. "Rick Glacier himself."

"Have any wanna-be Rick Glaciers been in here claiming to be the real thing?" I asked.

"Everyone wants to be Rick Glacier," she grinned.

"How you doing, Beats?"

"Just fine, Mister Glacier." She nodded to Mo, who sulked off to get the sissy I'd scared off another drink. "What can I help you with?"

"I was hoping to talk to you about a client," I told her. "Former client, someone murdered her."

"Now who would go and do a thing like that?" she asked sweetly.

"I've got a few thoughts on that, but I need to know which one's right." I looked around, the people in the booths all carried on their own conversations, no one watching us, no one listening. Or so it seemed. Someone was watching. In a place like this, someone always was. "Can we take this to your office?"

She nodded. "Concerned about eavesdroppers? Why Rick, I can't imagine what you're worried about."

"Your office?" I growled.

She nodded again, and with a wave signaled me to follow her through the door behind the bar. The hallway was narrow, and long and winding. At the end of each turn a massive, bulldozer of a man stood guard. Beats talked nonstop as we walked.

"It cost a small fortune for this hallway," she was saying, "because we designed it like a maze, so we had to knock out all the original walls to build it. We had to do all sorts of alterations to the foundation, you understand, and do it all without..." she stopped walking, touched her chin and thought for a moment, "prying eyes," she finished. Reached behind her and knocked on a door I hadn't noticed.

I heard the lock pull back and the door swung open to reveal a short little man wearing suspenders over a white shirt, a visor on his balding head.

"This is Peter," Beats introduced him, "my accountant. And he was just leaving," she added.

He left. We both went in. She locked the door behind her and crossed to the desk. The office was large and sparsely furnished. Most of the space was taken up by stacks of paperwork in various heights, an odd filing system by anyone's standards. I took a closer look at one: a spreadsheet.

"Don't worry about that," Beats said wistfully from the desk. "Even I don't know what any of it means. It's all just numbers on paper, something to do with taxes."

"I see," I said dryly.

"So what exactly did you want to talk to me about?"

"My client," I reminded her. "The dead one."

"Oh yes, of course, what about it?"

"Her. She was a woman and her name was Melanie Marx." I watched her reaction, there wasn't one. "Ring any bells?"

"Of course it does," she waved me off. "She and Sammy were regulars. If you're asking if I knew she was dead, the answer is yes."

I leaned against the wall and stared at her hard.

"I'm not here to find out if you knew she was dead," I told her. "I'm here to find out who got her that way."

She batted her eyelashes and looked shocked. "And what would make you think I know something like that?"

"Because," I shrugged myself off the wall and closed the distance between us, "you *do* know. You know everything that happens on the street. Don't you?"

"Well I…" she shook her head, huffing indignantly, "I don't know what to say."

"One of two words, babe, that's all you need to say. Delaney, or Coronado, that's all I want. One name."

"That's a very simplistic way of looking at it, Rick, in a manner of speaking they both got her killed."

I gave her a light slap on the cheek. Not hard enough to leave a mark, but enough to let her know I was serious.

"I don't need to hear that smart talk," I told her. "Who did it?"

"Fine," she spat, "I'll tell you what you want to know, but not until you learn how to treat a woman. It ain't slapping them around the first time they talk back."

"You're right, that's only half of it," I said. Pulled her up from the office chair and laid a kiss on those full lips. They resisted for only a split second, then parted and kissed me back.

She leaned back and looked up at me with those dark eyes, then left me standing there, crossed the room kicking stacks of paper over. Stopped and glanced back me, lips parted, a sultry look of desire playing across her beautiful face. I looked down at the papers scattered all around her, beneath her feet, and knew what she was playing at.

She'd made a paper mattress.

I was on her in flash. Kissing. Touching. Probing.

There was a knock at the door. It went unanswered.

She unbuckled my belt, kissing me as she shoved my pants down and took me in her hands. Her fingers slowly worked their way along the entire length then froze. She pushed away from me, her eyes wide with wonder when they confirmed what her hands had told her.

"My God," she said in a hoarse whisper, "I've never...."

"I know, babe," I smiled at her, "but it's made for more than just looking good."

That snapped her out of it. She dropped to her knees, her long dress dragging on the paperwork strewn beneath it, and took as much of me in her mouth as she could. Gagged. Tried harder. I smoothed her dark hair as she did.

I let her play with it for a few minutes, didn't want to cut her off and upset her. She was definitely enjoying herself. I wondered if she was trying to learn how to hold her breath longer and just practicing on me. But then she did a little something with her tongue and I wasn't thinking about anything anymore.

Finally she stood, shrugged off her dress, and then drew herself close to me. I gently laid her down on the paper, giving her small, pert breasts the attention they deserved before moving down to swirl my tongue inside her bellybutton. I left a trail of kisses along her smooth belly, ventured further down to the soft patch of hair between her thighs, and did some in depth exploration that had her squirming and moaning.

When she was primed and ready, I entered her missionary style, taking it slow and easy until her body adjusted to my size. She seemed to like it that way, didn't press for anything more adventurous, and I always like to accommodate a lady when it suits me. But I couldn't let her think I was soft so I picked up the rhythm and when the time was right, took her in long, heavy strokes that had her gasping for air as she spiraled over the edge.

I rode her through it, let my own thunder roll, then flopped onto my back and dragged in a much needed lungful of air. I went to light a smoke, remembered I was laying on a bed of paper, thought better of it and decided to do a little talking first.

"So," I panted, "Coronado?"

She nodded. She wasn't up to speaking yet. I looked at her, covered in beads of sweat, her body like some exotic creature. I didn't want it to be over so soon. But it was. I was running out of time.

"How did you know?" she finally said.

"Fifty-fifty guess," I said.

"What are you going to do to him?" she asked, curling her body so that her head was nestled close to my chest.

"I'm going to kill him and everyone around him," I told her. "What would you have me do?"

"It'll hurt my business," she said softly. "I'll lose thousands of dollars over it."

"What are you saying? You trying to buy me off?" I lifted myself off the floor and pulled on my pants. Looked down at her, still curled on the floor. "Rick Glacier isn't for sale," I growled.

I unlocked the door and walked out, letting it slam shut behind me with a sound that echoed through the narrow halls. Turned the corner walking fast. I had business to take care of. The killing kind of business. I just had one thing to decide.

A. Go straight to the Roxy, to hell with the package, kill Coronado with your bare hands if necessary. - flip to Chapter 13c.

B. Go home and get the package first, then go let Coronado have it. - flip to Chapter 13d.

CHAPTER 12C

I decided to pay a little visit to John Blonton, a femme and vet who worked as a gay call-boy out of his penthouse suite. I couldn't believe there were enough fags in town to keep him in the big money, but apparently there was.

I met him back in Sicily when he was getting laid by a General with a pretty wife at home and no real desire to go back to her. Eventually they were both outed after a shower session and got booted from the service. The General drank himself to death and Johnny boy went on to bigger and better things.

His apartment was in the good part of town, with marble sidewalks and men to answer the door and keep the riff-raff out. The door man looked at me, up and down, and I wondered if he wasn't half a Nancy himself, and then he let me pass.

I stopped at the front desk and asked for Mr. Blonton. The desk clerk was a pretty thing; plush all over. She would have been plenty of fun to roll around with. She gave me a shy smile as she called up for permission.

She got it, and I went up.

The elevator man opened the door for me when we reached the top, stepped out of the way and let me enter.

The apartment was massive, with light blazing in through a wall made entirely of windows. The floors were stone polished to a glass finish. There was music playing softly from somewhere out of sight. Piano, maybe. The furniture was all fashion and no comfort, the type you would expect to find in Johnny's apartment. It wasn't there to be used, just to be seen. All the action was in the bedroom.

"Well, well, Mister Glacier," I heard Blonton's feminine hiss from behind me, spun and saw him standing there in a robe. "To what do I owe this pleasure? Wait, don't tell me," he put out a dainty hand, raised it to my chest, "you've come to talk about my offer, all those years ago."

Years ago, way back in Sicily, when I had called him out as being queer as the day is long, he had offered to show me just how good he could work it. Just what I was missing with the ladies.

I thought about it. It had been a couple hours since I had gotten my rocks off. I could use a drink, too. What could it hurt? I'd try anything once. I'd let him get me off and then get my answers. Might be fun. No one would know.

"Yeah," I nodded, "That's why I'm here...."

(Wrong, Bitch. I can't believe this! This is *RICK FUCKING GLACIER!* Rick Glacier doesn't tap guys. He hits the ladies, Son. He's a man! And don't try to play it off with your friends like you *accidentally* picked the only one with a man as an option. You knew damn well how Glacier asks questions and what he does if he doesn't get answers. And I don't want to hear any shit about how having a guy sucking your dick doesn't make you gay. It does, you fucking putz. Only closet dwellers and convicts make that claim. Go back and make a different choice. And this time, pick a skirt, because Rick Glacier won't be acting out your perverse sexual fantasies anytime soon.)

CHAPTER 13A

I decided to go home and get my package before I hit the Joint. Madam Melvue had said he took all his boys and was holing up at the bar and I didn't want to try to take them all on with just my Luger. As sexy of a gun as it is.

I took a cab, promised the driver a buck if he was fast, and made it to my apartment in record time. I gave him another buck and told him to wait for me. Got out. He took off, waving the bill at me as he did.

You just couldn't trust Puerto Ricans.

But I had already known that.

I took the stairs five at a time. Got to the top. Unlocked the door. Grabbed the package. Back out.

The package was heavy, and I didn't feel much like walking, so I hitched a ride in yet another cab, thinking how much I would save by just buying my own, and rode in silence to the Joint. The place was locked up tight, or looked to be when the hack pulled up across the street. I didn't know what was happening inside, but I knew I wouldn't be getting in this way. Not through the front door. Not while it was still on its hinges.

"Get out," I told the cabby.

He looked at me queerly, I repeated myself, and then for good measure unwrapped the package and showed it to him.

He got out. Ran.

What lay on my lap after I had tossed the wax paper into the front seat was a Brown Automatic Rifle, five twenty-round magazines, and two boxes of shells. I could always count on old McEachern.

I lit a smoke, had a drink, and watched the bar. A cop came by with the cabby and I explained that it was actually my cab, I had never seen the guy before but it was obvious he was a raving lunatic or a drunk. The cop decided he was probably both, and dragged him away in handcuffs. I went back to sitting, drinking, smoking, and loading .30-06 shells into the magazine of my automatic rifle.

By about eight, the pile of spent smokes was nearly too high to step over to get out. I decided now was as good a time as any to get it over with. Melvue had said they would be moving tonight, but not when, and I figured if I hit my flask any harder, I'd be sleeping when they finally emerged.

I filled my pockets with magazines. Loaded one into the rifle. Jacked a shell into place. Got out and put my hat on. Crossed the street and knocked on the door.

No one answered.

I knocked again. Same result.

"That's what you get," I told myself, "when you try to be a nice guy."

I took three steps back and opened up with BAR. A full twenty rounds spent in a matter of seconds. Splinters danced from the hard wood as the heavy lead shattered the grains. I took a moment to reload, then gave the door a kick and all hell broke loose.

Someone had snuck out the side and they loosed a bullet that sung as it flew past my head. I turned right and gave him five rounds in the stomach, gutting him and sending him backwards like he had a chute tugging at him in a strong wind. Turned back and stepped inside. Two boys were leveling Tommy guns at me, so I let the other fifteen rounds go and chopped them up into bits small enough for a dog to snack on.

Reloaded, crossed around the bar. I heard a snap and turned and a meaty fellow was holding a pea shooter at me. The BAR spat and his head disappeared in a puff of red mist. Another pop and Mike was behind the bar, holding something that looked like a toy in his massive hand. I didn't want to but I stroked the trigger and opened his chest like a cavity search. Looked at him and sighed.

"No more Luger talks for you, old pal," I said.

A commotion to my right drew me, and I watched as a sea of whops emerged from the back room, holding an assortment of rifles, shotguns, pistols and clubs. The clubs seemed a bit old school, to me, but I laid them out just the same. Chopped three of them in half before the rifle ran dry.

The room erupted in a storm of snaps, pops and muzzle flashes. Shotguns boomed fast and angry. Rifles let out lead that pelted the walls around me. I dove back and made it behind the bar before the hot death struck where I had been standing. Reloaded and readied myself.

There were at least twenty that had poured out of the back room. I dealt with three. That left seventeen. That was a pretty big number. I was down to two magazines. Forty shots. Plus a few with the Luger, but not enough to do much with the little bullets. I needed something to even the odds. Ten against one would be fine. Seventeen was a stretch.

A clunk to my right and I looked and my eyes swelled. Someone had tossed a grenade. Not a friendly grenade either. A real, live, army grenade. Like the kind you read about crooks throwing in books but never really happens.

I was up and out and firing as I ran.

I took out two to my right. Three to my left. Tore one's shoulder off right in front of me. I was in a crowd now, it was harder to use the rifle. But it was even harder for them to shoot at me lest they hit their friends. I used the butt of the rifle and bludgeoned a guy's nose into his brain. Swung it like an axe and cracked another's neck like a twig. I was about to bite someone's ear off, not sure whose, when the grenade exploded and the world came crashing down around us.

Shrapnel fell five guys right out of the gate. Just shredded them and left them with more holes than an afghan. I lucked out and had a few human shields between me and the blast. The flame licked up and out and caught all the bottles on the wall behind it, feeding it propellant. The bottles exploded one by one, sending glass into mobsters who were now running in every direction.

I got a hold of my BAR, and mowed them down without mercy as they made for the door. There was a sound like thunder and I felt something heavy burrow into my shoulder. Spun to see Roger Delaney holding a service pistol of the M1911 type, the barrel smoking.

"It'll take more than that to take me down, Glacier," he growled.

"It'll take more than that just to make me curse, Delaney."

I turned the barrel of the rifle at him and hit the trigger. Nothing happened. He fired again, and blew chunks of plaster off the wall next me.

"Nice aim," I told him. Dropped the BAR. Pulled my Luger. "This sweet little baby's been waiting for you."

I sighted down the barrel and pulled the trigger. It jumped just a fraction of an inch. I pulled it three more times, watching as the bullets smacked into his chest with wet sounds. Blood began to spool out from the holes.

He fell.

I left him there.

Outside there was nothing but the sound of fire crackling and sirens howling. I sat down at the curb, lit a smoke, and took the clip out of my Luger. They'd be wanting it for evidence. Decided to finish my flask. It went down harsh but was worth it. I set the Luger down next to the clip, stuck my smoke in my teeth and put my hands up.

The first squad car to arrive was driven by Hugo McEachern, and he wasn't a happy man.

"God Damn You Glacier!" he roared.

"Please don't use language like that," I smiled stupidly at him. "It hurts my delicate sensibilities."

"You're gonna be in a world of hurt over this one, Glacier," he wagged a sausage of a finger in front of my face. "And don't think you'll get out of it just because you're my pal. I told you not to make a mess," he reminded me.

"I told you it would be cleaner my way," I reminded him.

"How is this less messy?" he showcased the carnage as he asked it.

"Roger Delaney was about to start a turf war," I explained. "He was ready to move on Coronado. He also killed Melanie Marx."

"So you did all this to protect Coronado? And revenge the lady?"

"The latter, actually," I said. "But not revenge. Justice. Coronado kidnapped Sammy Marx, he's got him holed up at the Roxy for safe keeping."

"How do you know he's at the Roxy? And I thought you said he didn't want to be found."

"He doesn't," I sighed, "but only because he's queer for the piano player. He's at the Roxy because Missus Marx got wacked, that's the only place Coronado would feel he was safe."

"If all that's true, Glacier, I might be able to clear this with the DA," he said, rubbing his face. Firefighters pulled up and started their work. "But it's a long shot."

I got up and climbed into the back of his car. He took my piece and put it in a paper bag. Stuffed it in the glove compartment.

"Try not to kill anyone for five minutes," he sneered at me.

I tried it. Didn't seem like much fun.

(Continue to Chapter 14)

CHAPTER 13B

I didn't have time to get the package. I had wasted too much time with the Madam.

The hack grunted when I told him to take me to the Joint, nodded and pulled off the curb. I pulled a pint from my pocket and downed a swig, processing information. I didn't have the package and that presented a problem, but for all I knew in the time it would take to pick it up, Delaney could explode the whole town. I needed a plan.

I lit a smoke and drank some more. The cabby was eyeing my bottle, so I gave him a nip and he sped up. Handed it back and I took another hit. The city was a blur moving past me. I settled back in my seat and thought hard.

I had my Luger on me. She was a sweet little pistol but not enough against the kind of numbers I would be facing. I took a drink, looked at the bottle in my hand, and got an idea.

The night was dead when the cab stopped at the Joint. The place was even more so. Stitched up tight as a girdle on a thick dame, with no one in sight. The shutters were drawn and around the edges small slivers of light shown through. I tossed a two dollar bill at the driver and got out.

Up ahead, straight across the street from the bar, was an old broken down truck with a wooden fence around its bed. I checked it out. Looked like as a good a spot as any, so I laid out all my clips right there. Laid them next to each other in one neat line. Kept the Luger in its holster. Tore off a bit of my sleeve, dowsed it in liquor and then shoved it into the bottle. Took it back out and had one more taste. Put it back in.

I was ready.

I darted across the street. Hugged up against the outside wall and looked left and then right. Crabbed along the wall and turned the corner. Kept close to that wall, too, and made it to the back door. It was locked up tight. I didn't care much either way.

I shook what was left of my pint, pulled out my lighter, sparked it, and touched the flame to the cloth wick. Took two steps back and threw the bottle at the hard wooden door. The bottle shattered like a glass snowball, shards exploding out in a pretty little halo. The liquor inside dowsed the wick and the flames caught, licking up the door and igniting the entire thing.

I took off around the corner. Across the street. Behind the truck. It would take a few minutes, I knew. I knocked a Lucky from the pack and lit it. Settled back for the wait. I could already see smoke billowing up into the night, black and fierce. The roof glowed slightly from the fire raging behind it. I waited some more.

Someone was shouting. I heard bolts moving behind the door. More shouting. The door opened. I leveled my Luger and waited for a mark. The first one out was the bartender, Mike, my old buddy. I didn't feel too bad about putting two 9 mm's into his chest. I had known him a long time, and knew I wouldn't miss him much. He was pressed forward by a crowd of gangsters as his legs went out. I fired again. Again and again. Just fired into the mass of flesh until the Luger went dry. Expelled the clip and snapped another one in.

The crowd had started to unfurl outside the club. They were looking around as they did, stepping over the bodies of four of their brethren. I shot one in the head, saw a puff of black rise as he fell. Tracked left and put three bullets into a monster next to him. He fell, exposing a new target behind him. I shot that one but he didn't go down. Reloaded and put two more in his chest, his dark body finally lay at rest next to his friend's.

The night exploded into a sea of pops and cracks as the remaining hoods opened fire on me. The wood around me splintered and rocked with the impacts. Sparks showered out as bullets ricocheted off the metal body.

I ducked back and waited for the onslaught to end. It didn't. They just kept right on firing. As one would run dry another would continue to fire. It was all I could do to hug the side of the truck and try to make myself small. That didn't work real well, and I got hit in the shoulder. Then one of them got an idea, dropped down on his knees and shot at my legs. The bullets tore through my flesh, bouncing off my bones.

I had to move. It was suicide to stay there.

I gloved around to the front of the truck, crouched low, behind the wheel well. Popped up and shot a youngster twice in the gut, then ducked back around the truck. The gunfire intensified. I looked up to see that one of them had come around the back holding a shotgun. He fired and took half my face off, blood erupting and covering my chest, the ground, my legs.

I felt pavement against my back, then my head slapped hard on the solid, cold concrete sidewalk and I looked up

through a haze of blood and smoke and saw a few stars twin-
kling way up there in heaven.

"Lemme through," someone was saying, cursing in vul-
garities not fit for the public. "I said let me through!"

Suddenly a black form hovered over me, blocking out the
stars. It was Roger Delaney, and as I focused in I saw he was
smiling.

"You think one punk with a Luger can take me out?" he
asked, didn't wait for an answer. Instead I felt something cold
and round touch my forehead, and he pulled the trigger.

I didn't hear the bang.

(Holy Mother of the Virgin Mary! I am sick to fucking *death*
of you! Forget the package? Sure, why the fuck not? Just go
into a war zone with a Luger and a few clips. That'll work.
Next time why don't you ask if they'll all stand in a neat
little line, so you can kill three or four of them with a single
shot? Wouldn't that be helpful? I'm so pissed right now I'm
tempted to tell you once and for all to fuck off. But I won't.
Go back and make the right decision, because you should
have known what it was all along. And maybe learn to count.
Thirty gangsters against twenty-something bullets, fuck man,
calculators aren't all that expensive. Shit Bird.)

CHAPTER 13C

I didn't have time to get my package, I had wasted too much of it with Beats. I hit the street and hailed a cab and told him to take me to the Roxy. He did, and as he did I sat and smoked and thought about some things.

I needed that package, I grimaced, but while I was wasting time getting it Coronado could burn half the city down. No. I needed something else. I needed something big to take down a good swath and then I could pick off the stragglers with the Luger. But what?

The cab lurched around a corner, too fast, and I had my idea.

A block away I told the hack to slow down. Then stop. Then I grabbed him by the shoulder, stuck my Luger against his head and calmly explained I would need to borrow his ride.

"Mister," he stammered, "you don't want no trouble with the law, now do you?"

"I were you," I said, "I'd be more worried about you getting into trouble with my sexy little pistol here."

That seemed to make sense to him, and he opened his door and took off at a triathlon pace. I had never seen anyone run like that, but the blacks always seemed exceptionally fast.

I got out of the back and got into the front. Pressed my piece back into the holster and dropped the car into drive. Then I closed the last half of the block at an incredibly irresponsible speed, at least fifty, and as the Roxy came into view, cold and black and looming against the curb, I gunned it and pulled hard on the wheel and jumped the curb and slammed through the front doors.

Three meaty hoods stood in front of it, and they didn't have a good time of being crushed and sheered and wrapped in two as the cab barreled into them and threw them through the door. One skipped across the slick floors and took out Maxie's grand piano up on stage.

I put the car in park and got out. Pulled my Luger and waited. Nothing happened.

"Mister Vito Coronado," I boomed. "I would like a word."

My voice echoed and played off the walls of the empty club. Then died out as it lost its rhythm and fell to the floor. Still nothing happened.

"Well," I grumbled, "this isn't exactly what I had in mind."

Just then the room exploded in a hailstorm of leaden fury. It seemed like shooters were everywhere. They must have surrounded me while I was standing lamely by the car, waiting for what I didn't know. Now I was squarely in the kill box with no way out that I could see.

I dropped to the floor but not fast enough to keep from getting clipped in both shoulders. The wounds burned as the hot bullets slowly cooled inside my flesh. I sighted under the car and saw at least sixty legs, thirty pairs. I had to even the odds a bit.

From under the cab I shot out a pair of ankles. Then sent their owner to the great beyond as he landed, his face level line with mine. A 9 mil cut through his throat and blood erupted across the floor like a long red gash. I followed the same procedure with three more before they got the idea and pulled the legs up. Some went onto the stage, some ducked behind the bar, I guessed some sat up on stools.

I was out of targets and pinned down. But the firing stopped abruptly and I heard a voice call out, loud, angry and self assured.

"Well, well," Vito Coronado's voice came, "if it isn't the talented Mister Glacier. Seems you've been humbled a bit."

"You just keep talking, Vito," I called. "Once I know where you're at, I'll pick up this car and just toss it at you."

That made him laugh.

"Defiant to the end, I see. Do you think, maybe, we could work this thing out? I'm a reasonable man. And you've proven to me that you could be an incredible asset. Everyone needs a man who knows how to get answers. I'll tell you what: you come onto the payroll. What's your day rate?"

"Too rich for you," I told him, squirmed under the car. It was a tight space and my bulk wasn't working well in it. I was trying to think my way out of the situation, out from under this car, and somehow into a position where I could shoot that smugness right off Coronado's face.

"Whatever it is," he replied, "double it. Hell, triple it. I don't care. I'll pay it. Otherwise, I'm afraid you won't survive much longer."

I heard sirens off in the distance and knew I wouldn't live to see them arrive. Coronado had every right to shoot me right there, and enough cops on the payroll to do it without any right. I had to do *something*.

"Alright," I sighed, didn't see any other way, "two hundred a day."

"That's very expensive, Mister Glacier."

"I'm worth it."

"Fine," he chuckled, "that's just fine Glacier. Now you crawl your way out from under that car, and we'll shake on it."

I slid myself out from under the car and stood. Got a look at Coronado. He was standing up on stage, grinning wickedly. He had the look in his eyes that dogs got just before a meal. He motioned to someone and I felt something hard hit my back and I doubled over. My Luger was taken from me and I was pulled back up with my arms pinned behind me.

Coronado crossed the room with all the confidence of a triumphant General. He had a swagger about him that said he was in complete control, which he was. He wore a white suit with a black shirt. No tie. With shiny shoes that glistened as he stepped over pools of blood to approach me.

"Did you really think I would hire *you*?" he asked. "Look at you."

He waved a manicured hand over my chest, riddled with holes, blood pouring to the floor in currents stronger than the Hudson.

He nodded to someone, and then said to me, "I'm not even going to dignify your existence by shooting you myself. Because it would be beneath me. I don't kill cockroaches; I have people do it for me. Thus is the case here."

He turned and strode away in that thick swagger of his, waved a palm over his shoulder and said, "Get this cleaned up, please."

Then I felt something cold on my temple and someone pulled the trigger and the world went white.

(I... I... I don't even know what to say at this point. I'm completely *fucking* dumbfounded. Were you born this stupid, or do you practice? I gotta be honest, the only thing stopping me from telling you to fuck off and never read my books again is my own passionate greed. Even cash from the stupidest motherfucker in the world, which you are, still spends the same as anyone else's. So go back and make the right decision. There's only two choices, for Christ's sake! Oh, and fuck you.)

CHAPTER 13D

I needed my package. I told the cabby my address and he nodded and took me there. Then he took three dollars for the service. I wondered if they were raising the price every time I went. I paid him and gave him an extra five to hang out until I came back. He took it and smiled and as soon as my feet touched pavement his pressed the pedal and I was lucky to get out of the door before the cab had taken my torso off.

There was a reason no one trusted the blacks.

I took the stairs up to my apartment eight at a time. Hurling myself up them, using the railing like a pole vault. Got to my door. Opened it. Went in. Got my package. Went out. Went back in. Grabbed a bottle. Back out. I hit the street less than three minutes after entering the building. Hailed yet another hack. Got in. Barked, "The Roxy."

I used the ride to chain smoke, tossing the butts out the window, and drink the majority of my bottle. The cabby looked into the rearview, thirsty for my whiskey and I let him look. Kept right on drinking and smoking and thinking.

We got to the Roxy and he pulled up onto the sidewalk. Literally. He hopped the curb and stopped the car on the concrete. I looked at him and he shrugged.

"That'll be two seventy-five," he said.

I handed him what was left of the bottle, because if I finished it I'd be hard pressed to walk let alone shoot straight, and told him to get out. He looked at me lamely. I unwrapped the package and let him take a look at a genuine Browning Automatic Rifle, five twenty-round magazines and two boxes of ammo.

He got out. Ran.

I loaded up the magazines. Put four in my pockets and one in the rifle. Jacked a shell in the chamber and got out.

The Roxy was closed up tight as a drum. Three mountains guarded the door. It was the first time I had ever heard of the Roxy closed after dark. Of course, it was only the second time I been to the Roxy. I kept to the shadows around the halos from the lampposts, and got within twenty feet before one of them saw me.

"Hey, you can't be here," he shouted and then lost the upper half of his body in a murderous spray of .30-06 rounds. His friends were caught in the sweep and fell where they stood, or several feet away depending on the direction of the rifle mussel.

I tried the door. Unlocked. Coronado must have thought his muscle was enough to stop me. He was wrong.

I went in and spotted three guys making for the door. Peashooters in their hands. I chopped them up like liver. Leaving bits of them to be collected later by the cops. There was a muffled scream as one of the cocktail girls took off for an exit. I let her go and kept walking.

Two more Johns came out of the John. I nailed them both up high, taking them apart at the neck. A shot rang out behind me. I spun, rifle blaring, and ripped through a small group of gangsters, their bullet riddled bodies performing a macabre little jig as I continued to fill them full of lead until the last one fell.

This was going too easy. I couldn't be taking them apart without some serious fireworks. If Coronado was ready for war, he should have had more....

A swarm came out from behind the bar. Thirty men, easily. Like locusts. They came around, over, and under the bar, weapons trained and ready.

I pulled the trigger but nothing happened. I was dry and had forgotten to reload.

I ran.

The ground, walls, ceiling, everything around me exploded as it was pelted with hundreds of bullets. I made it to the back of the room and turned a corner, reloading, waiting and hoping they didn't come from the other side of the hall. I saw two try to make it into the corridor and I opened up, slaying them right where they stood. Then took off running in the opposite direction.

Someone fired at my back, I spun and returned fire, felling an oak of a man. I took him out at the knees and he went down hard. I didn't stop to yell "timber." A left turn and a right turn. Reloading as I went.

Coronado's office. I kicked in the door and found him sitting on a couch, looking dapper and a little bored with a cocktail waitress riding him. She glanced over her shoulder, didn't seem surprised that someone had been invited to join in on the action. Then her eyes lowered and she saw the Browning and realized my business wasn't with her. She let out a shriek, jumped off of Vito, her generous breasts bobbing up and down as she scampered past me and into the hall. I gave her rear a pat as she passed.

The wall next to me jumped. I fired right and clipped a scrawny little hood with a service revolver. Turned left and emptied the rifle into a pair of micks the size of tractor tires. Looked back and felt something hard hit my chest.

Vito was holding a shotgun, the barrel smoking. I looked down and saw tiny little dots starting to bleed. My right shoulder was filled with them. I shrugged and reloaded the BAR. He fired again. This time I lurched backward and hit the wall on the other side of the hall. Fired left, killed a guy. Fired right, killed another one.

"It'll take more than some punk with a machine gun to bring me down," Coronado spat.

"It'll take more than a crook with a scatter gun just to make me upset," I replied. Raised the BAR and opened up. Fifteen rounds in a few seconds. The entire office was a kill zone. Coronado jumped and convulsed as the bullets eviscerated his entire body. Arms flew off. Legs crumbled. Head popped like a cherry blossom.

I left him there, a steaming heap of flesh and shattered bone. I still had to get out alive.

I made a series of right turns. Emptied my last clip. Ended up back at the office. Made some left turns. Pulled my Luger. Ended up back at the office.

"Is this a maze?" I muttered to myself.

I decided to try a combination of lefts and rights and found my way out. Back to the club.

The place was a wreck. Two good ol' boys turned Tommy guns on me and I expertly shot each in the eye. They dropped like bags of potatoes.

I made for the door.

I felt a sting in my left shoulder, spun and put a bullet in the throat of a wop holding a pistol. Blood poured out like a faucet. I turned and kept on for the door. Got hit in the leg and dispatched the shooter with a 9 mil to the chest. Gave him one more in the face for good measure.

I stepped outside. There was a crowd forming. I could hear sirens wailing in the distance. I remembered something and went back inside.

Three hoods ran past me. They didn't seem interested in me. Must have found what was left of their boss and figured they would seek out other job opportunities.

I went behind the bar and found the trap door I knew would be there. Opened it and went down, my Luger ready. The staircase opened up into a cellar filled with beer and wine and liquor of assorted sizes, tastes and colors. I grabbed a bottle of whiskey, popped the top and had myself a good draw on it. Then set it down for later and kept moving. At the back of the cellar I found what I was looking for.

Sammy Marx was curled up like a scared little kitten. Shaking. I got closer and saw his pants were wet from where he'd urinated on himself. I told him to get up.

"Who're you?" he stammered.

"I'm Rick Glacier," I told him. "Your wife hired me."

"Melanie? Is she here?" He looked around like he expected to find her hiding behind one of the crates.

"No," I grabbed his shoulder hard and pulled him back the way I'd come. "Vito killed her last night. Now I'm taking you to the cops."

We went up the stairs, grabbing my bottle on the way, out the door and met a group of cops holding very serious looking guns and pointing them at our chests.

"Wait!" I heard Hugo call from behind them. "Wait! That's Glacier! Don't shoot."

He came through the crowd as they lowered their weapons, a weary look on his face.

"How are you doing today, McEachern?"

"How am I doing?" he huffed. "How am I doing? You shot up half the city, how do you think I'm doing?"

"You're welcome," I said. "Coronado was about to start a gang war. He killed Melanie Marx, too. I stopped the whole damn city from burning down."

"And gave the whole thing to Delaney," he reminded me.

"Here," I pushed Sammy Marx at him. "That's Delaney's banker. And I bet he'll testify this time, won't you?"

"Yes, sir," he nodded, "anything you want."

"Good," I snarled, "cuz if you don't I'll give you the same treatment as Coronado."

Hugo sighed. "It might just pass. The DA's wanted these two jokers out of the way a long time. That's the only reason it might fly." He pointed at the Luger in my hand. "I'm gonna need your piece," he told me, "but you can keep the bottle."

(Continue to Chapter 14)

CHAPTER 14

I put out my cigarette and sighed. The whiskey tasted nutty as I sipped it. It felt good as it went down, burning all the way. Behind me the city was a sea of honking horns, flashing lights, and bustling pedestrians. I didn't look out the window, just stared at my door.

I had a case under my belt now. That was supposed to mean more clients. Maybe they didn't like how I closed cases. Getting my client killed. Getting her husband arrested. Burning through my day rate faster than I earned it. Laying it to every skirt along the way.

What did that make me? Efficient? A hero? A crook with a PI license? All of the above?

I figured it just made me Rick Glacier. No reason to over think it.

There was a slight, soft tapping on my door. I called for them to come in. The door opened and a red head looking like something out of a pulp novel walked in. She had on a short dress, split along her left thigh. She held a purse high under her arm. A cigarette hung provocatively from her lips.

"Mister Glacier?" she asked.

"That's what it says on the door," I pointed to my name. "What can I do for you?"

She sucked in a deep breath and held it. Her lungs expanded and drew attention to her breasts. She was ten feet away, on the other side of my desk, but I felt their presence and I wanted them closer. In my hands, if possible. Mouth would be even better.

She let out her breath in a sigh. "I need your help," she said.

I had a decision to make....

ABOUT THE AUTHOR

Bill Pryst is the first of what will undoubtedly be a string of best-selling writers to work with Finnean Nilsen Projects. He lives in his car with his girlfriend[s] and works as a fried foods salesman and occasionally as a sex-offender decoy. In addition to writing, his interests are spelunking, garbage diving, braiding women's hair, football, alcohol binges, and homemade pornography. If you would like to reach Bill and tell him how awesome he is, or if you are a consenting female under the age of sixty-five that would like to offer him your body, you can contact him at: billf_ckingpryst@live.com.

ABOUT THE PRODUCTION COMPANY

Finnean Nilsen Projects is a production company for books, movies, games, and life saving/improving inventions. Consisting of two equally talented brothers (of which I'm the more attractive, obviously), it was founded in close cooperation with their mother, who swears off any responsibility for their actions and reminds you that it is all the fault of their fathers and not their upbringing. If you would like to send them money, or if you are an author as amazing as Bill Pryst (you're not) you can contact them at: finnilpro@live.com

ABOUT THE TYPE

Originally, the type for this book was to be designed by the artist and brilliant physicist Gaylord McIntyre. He envisioned an entirely revolutionary new letter system. Based on a series of dots and dashes not unlike Morse code, it was going to change the way people read, thought, and possibly cause seizures. Unfortunately, just as he was about to deliver what would have undoubtedly been his masterpiece; he was trampled to death by a stampede of rampaging water buffalo. We decided to settle on Times New Roman.

ABOUT THE WEATHER

It's crazy, right?

P.S.

A MESSAGE FROM THE AUTHOR

Dear Fans,

It is my sincerest hope that you enjoyed reading this story as much as I enjoyed writing it. I just ask that if you did enjoy it, tell a friend, and write a review online. But don't give anyone your copy, let them buy their own. I need the money. Alimony is expensive.

It's called hookin' a brother up.

And while you're at it, how about hooking up our brothers and sisters in uniform serving abroad and buy them a copy. Don't send them yours, it's been tainted. Buy a new one and send them that. And make sure they don't pass that shit around. Someone should buy each of them a copy and send it out. And no reading it before they send it. This whole passing a book from one person to another shit needs to stop.

In fact, after the book is read it should be destroyed and a new one purchased. This is serious. I already said I need the money. Don't feel bad about using it for kindling, just burn the fucker and buy a new one. I like the sound of that. Buy five and burn four, I don't give a shit, just keep buying.

On a serious level, we need to stimulate this fucking economy. Buying my book puts money in my pocket and I'll spend it on women and drinking, and on drinking women. I think they call it trickle down economics. Spend money to make money. See, I'm a big spender. You pay for my book: I'll keep a girl in college. Because strippers are all using their tips to pay for college, and that's a noble fucking cause if you ask me.

Sincerely,
Bill Pryst

Check out the Multiple-Choice Paranormal Phenomena...

CREPUSCULAR LIGHT

It's like Twilight, only it doesn't suck.

Brandt Mako is 100% sure he's a fairy, he just doesn't know if that makes him a mythological creature, or gay. But to find out, he'll have to navigate his way through the vampires, werewolves, changelings and Greek Gods, the genetically evolved race of human/ animal hybrids, the witches and warlocks and time-traveling highlanders and cyborgs with enhanced, steel hard, extra-large, vibrating sex organs.
Sound like a little much?
WRONG!
Because this time it's not just sex, it's gay sex, it's consensual (mostly) and you're calling the shots. In this Multiple-Choice Paranormal Romance, see if you can find out what Brandt really is and how he likes it. But most importantly of all, let's show the world that not only vampires suck...

Available anywhere Twilight is not.